Silvers Is Tarnished

"What do you know about a reporter named Clayton Silvers?" Frank Hardy asked Joe's friend Darryl, an intern at the *Bayport Times*.

"Take 'Em Down Silvers? I know the good and the bad." Darryl handed Frank a folder of articles. "Silvers brought down mobsters as well as crooked politicians and corporations. Nothing and nobody was too big for him to tackle. He cost some powerful folks some serious green. . . . Guess he made some, too."

Frank looked up. "What do you mean?"

Darryl pulled out a clipping. " 'Silvers Is Tarnished,' " Darryl quoted without looking at the paper. " 'Well-known reporter accused of taking bribes.' "

"Bribes for what?" Callie Shaw asked.

"They found proof that people had paid him to go after their opponents or business rivals," Darryl said. "They'd even given him tips and leads. He made their rivals look bad, so *his* clients looked good."

"This is too wild!" Joe exclaimed. "How are we going to tell Aunt Gertrude that her old, best friend . . . is a crook?"

The Hardy Boys Mystery Stories

#105 The Smoke Screen Mystery
#107 Panic on Gull Island
#108 Fear on Wheels
#109 The Prime-Time Crime
#110 The Secret of Sigma Seven
#114 The Case of the Counterfeit Criminals
#124 Mystery with a Dangerous Beat
#133 Crime in the Kennel
#139 The Search for the Snow Leopard
#140 Slam Dunk Sabotage
#141 The Desert Thieves
#143 The Giant Rat of Sumatra
#147 Trial and Terror
#148 The Ice-Cold Case
#149 The Chase for the Mystery Twister
#150 The Crisscross Crime

#151 The Rocky Road to Revenge
#152 Danger in the Extreme
#153 Eye on Crime
#154 The Caribbean Cruise Caper
#155 The Hunt for the Four Brothers
#156 A Will to Survive
#157 The Lure of the Italian Treasure
#158 The London Deception
#159 Daredevils
#160 A Game Called Chaos
#161 Training for Trouble
#162 The End of the Trail
#163 The Spy That Never Lies
#164 Skin & Bones
#165 Crime in the Cards
#166 Past and Present Danger
The Hardy Boys Ghost Stories

Available from MINSTREL Books

THE HARDY BOYS®

166

PAST AND PRESENT DANGER

FRANKLIN W. DIXON

A MINSTREL® BOOK

Published by POCKET BOOKS

New York   London   Toronto   Sydney   Singapore

This book is a work of fiction. Names, characters, places and incidents are products of the author's imagination or are used fictitiously. Any resemblance to actual events or locales or persons, living or dead, is entirely coincidental.

A MINSTREL PAPERBACK Original

 A Minstrel Book published by
POCKET BOOKS, a division of Simon & Schuster, Inc.
1230 Avenue of the Americas, New York, NY 10020

Copyright © 2001 by Simon & Schuster, Inc.

Front cover illustration by Jeff Walker

ISBN: 0-7434-0660-5

First Minstrel Books printing March 2001

10 9 8 7 6 5 4 3 2 1

THE HARDY BOYS MYSTERY STORIES is a trademark of Simon & Schuster, Inc.

THE HARDY BOYS, A MINSTREL BOOK and colophon are registered trademarks of Simon & Schuster, Inc.

Printed in the U.S.A.

Contents

 1 *Out of the Blue*   1
 2 *Old Friends, New Enemies*   5
 3 *Tips and Tales*   14
 4 *Hard Headlines*   26
 5 *Dangerous Curves*   35
 6 *Nowhere to Go but Down*   46
 7 *Tall Stories*   56
 8 *Big Brother Is Watching*   66
 9 *Invasion*   76
10 *Nowhere Is Safe*   84
11 *"SEARCH"*   99
12 *Escape*   112
13 *Program for Destruction*   120
14 *Ground Zero*   126
15 *Subject Neutralized*   136
16 *All Clear*   145

PAST AND PRESENT DANGER

1 Out of the Blue

"You think we'll survive this?" seventeen-year-old Joe Hardy asked his older brother as he felt the muscles in his back tense up.

"I don't know." Frank Hardy stood grinning, surrounded by shopping bags. They were everywhere. "They've got us outnumbered four to one. It does look hopeless."

"It wouldn't be, if you two would stop procrastinating and load those bags," a stern voice insisted.

Frank and Joe smiled sheepishly. The voice belonged to their ever-efficient aunt Gertrude, their father's only sister. "It's four o'clock, and we still have three more stops to make before dinner."

The two brothers quietly groaned and finished loading the shopping bags in through the rear of their custom van. The boys often used the van to chase down crooks, but things had been quiet lately, as if all criminals had taken a holiday.

They couldn't help feeling a little disappointed, as this was the second day of their weeklong school break and they had hoped to spend it doing something—anything—more exciting than shopping.

It was a beautiful early fall day, perfect for biking, skateboarding—not for playing errand boys.

"Hey, Frank, Joe, what's up?" Tony Prito called out as he cruised by in his car. "See you down at Mr. Pizza later?"

"Not likely," Joe replied. "We've got more . . . *important* things to do."

Tony grinned. "Yeah, I can see that. Later."

"This wouldn't be bad if it were just down time between cases," Frank said. "But things have been too quiet lately."

Joe nodded. .

"I'm extremely happy you two are not involved in any murder and mayhem," said their aunt. She crossed several items off her list of errands. "It's bad enough Fenton courts danger, without his sons following suit."

Fenton Hardy, the boys' father, was a well-known and successful private investigator. It seemed as if his skills had rubbed off on the boys. Robbers, kidnappers, and saboteurs—Frank and Joe had tackled them all and with tremendous success.

"If only something would happen," Joe continued. He stepped over to a sidewalk newspaper dispenser and purchased a paper. The headline was in bold black type.

" 'City Council wants to bring more business to Bayport,' " Joe read out loud. "Our senator is lobbying for better ecological management of our shoreline. As I said, nothing earth-shaking."

"Senator Ogilvy is a good man," Aunt Gertrude declared. "I volunteered in his last campaign. He really cares about his constituents. In fact, he spends more time here than he does in Washington."

Frank Hardy shrugged his shoulders. "That's great, Aunt Gertrude," he said, "but a lot of politicians say and do anything to get elected."

"Well, not our senator, he—" Suddenly Aunt Gertrude glanced at the big clock on top of a store down the street. "Oh my, it's later than I thought, and we still have a lot to do before dinner."

Joe winked at Frank. "So maybe we should skip the rest of the list," he said.

Aunt Gertrude gave her nephew a look that said that was not an option.

"Okay, okay," Joe said sheepishly. "Scratch that idea." He walked around to the side of the van to hold the door for his aunt. "Okay, Aunt Gertrude," Joe said. "Let's get this show on the road."

Joe looked around. Where was his aunt? She was no longer standing behind the van. Movement caught his eye, and he turned to see his aunt running down the street. "Aunt Gertrude, where are you going?" Joe called out.

"What's up?" Frank asked.

Joe pointed to their aunt, who was now half a block away, in front of the mini mall they had just left. "I've never seen her run like that before," Joe said.

Frank grabbed his brother by the arm and took off after her. He thought he knew what had caused his aunt's running off. Then Joe spotted what Frank had seen.

Just beyond Aunt Gertrude three men were fighting. As the brothers drew closer it became clear that two of the men, one blond and one dark-haired, were attacking the third one. The two men then started to drag the third by the arms toward a white van parked at the curb.

Before Frank and Joe could catch up to their aunt, she had reached the men. The dark-haired one, tall and lean, had just raised his hand above the victim's head. Joe spotted a blackjack in the attacker's hand, ready to come down hard. That was when Aunt Gertrude shocked the boys for the second time. She reached up and quickly grabbed the man's arm, and held on with all her might.

But the man was strong, and the boys knew that it was only a matter of seconds before he'd break her grasp—and the first thing he'd strike would be her.

2 Old Friends, New Enemies

Frank and Joe put on a burst of speed, just as the attacker lowered his arm and Aunt Gertrude bit his hand. This caused the man to drop the blackjack.

The victim, a man with dark brown skin and short cropped hair, who was still on the sidewalk, took advantage of Aunt Gertrude's actions and focused on his other attacker, tripping him and sending him crashing to the pavement. The victim then tried to help Gertrude Hardy by grabbing her assailant around the legs.

Again, the man proved to be too strong. He kicked out and struck the victim a mean blow to the face while at the same time shoving Aunt Gertrude up against the van. The second assailant pushed up to his feet and was getting set to kick the victim. That was when Frank and Joe arrived.

Joe leaped and landed on the blond attacker while Frank jumped between the dark-haired man and their aunt. "Back off!" he shouted. The assailant only grinned wickedly as he swung a large fist at Frank's face.

The older Hardy ducked the swing and fired three rapid blows to the man's midsection. The attacker stumbled back, momentarily stunned and surprised. As Frank stepped in to deliver another blow, the man recovered enough to grab Frank's arm, elbow him in the jaw, and flip him over his shoulder.

Frank landed with a thud, the wind knocked out of him.

Joe had managed to wrestle himself on top of the other man and was about to deliver a right cross when he felt a sharp pain in his side. He was kicked by the man Frank had been fighting. The blow sent Joe spilling off his opponent, gasping for breath. He and his brother could only watch as the two men jumped into the white van. A third person, the unseen driver, threw the vehicle in gear and sped off. In seconds it was gone.

A crowd had begun to gather, and some people offered to help.

"Are you boys badly hurt?" Aunt Gertrude asked. She knelt between Frank and Joe as they rose up on their elbows.

"Just my pride," Joe replied, pushing himself to his feet.

Frank moaned slightly. "I think he hurt me a little bit more than that." Aunt Gertrude looked alarmed. "I'm really okay," he said, consoling her. He did wince slightly as he got to his knees, though. "Honest."

"Good," she said. Then she checked on the victim. "Are you all right?" she asked, the concern showing in her voice.

The man rubbed his jaw tenderly. "I guess so," he said slowly. Then he stared at Aunt Gertrude, and a stunned expression fell across his face. "I don't believe it. Spitfire, what are you doing here?"

Aunt Gertrude beamed, then blushed as she realized the boys and several onlookers were staring at her.

"Spitfire?" Frank and Joe said in unison.

Aunt Gertrude frowned as her whole face turned bright pink. "Boys, uh . . . this is Mr. Clayton Silvers, a friend of mine."

"An *old* friend," Mr. Silvers corrected enthusiastically. "We went to high school together."

"Nice to meet you," Frank said. He rose to his feet and extended his right hand to Mr. Silvers.

"I can call the police on my cell phone," one bystander offered.

"No, thank you," Clayton Silvers said quickly. "I'm okay."

"Spitfire?" Joe said, not wanting to let go of an obviously awkward situation.

Aunt Gertrude picked up her purse from the sidewalk and removed a handkerchief. "No one has called me that in years," she said. She gingerly dabbed at a cut on Clayton Silvers's lip.

Joe glanced at Frank, then back to his aunt. "Spitfire?" he repeated.

"We gave her that name because— Ow!" Clayton Silvers jerked away from Gertrude Hardy. "You trying to mend my wounds, or open them up?"

"Just hold still, Clayton," Gertrude Hardy told him.

"As I was just about to say. I—"

"Don't you dare, Clayton Aloysius Silvers!"

Clayton exchanged a mischievous look with Joe. "But why not? You used to be proud of that name. You *earned* it. I think the boys—"

Aunt Gertrude's nostrils flared. "You open your mouth, and I'll—"

"See what I mean?"

"Right now I think we need to deal with the question of who those men were," Frank said, taking the heat off his aunt. "Why were they attacking you, Mr. Silvers?"

Joe noticed a fast change in Clayton Silvers's attitude. But it vanished as quickly as it had appeared.

"Muggers," Clayton replied evenly. "I assume you have them here in Bayport just like anywhere."

"Did they take your money or wallet?" Joe asked.

"No," Clayton replied, not even checking his pockets. "So let's forget about it, okay?"

"But we should report it to the police," Frank said.

"Absolutely," Aunt Gertrude added. "In fact, Fenton often works with the authorities, and I'm sure—"

"No," Clayton replied more strongly than necessary. "I'd rather not."

Gertrude Hardy studied her old friend. "Are you here on a story?" she asked. Once again, Clayton Silvers appeared momentarily uncomfortable.

"A story?" Frank asked.

"Clayton is a crime reporter on a big Washington newspaper," Aunt Gertrude replied.

"Crime reporter?" Joe's interest was piqued. "Great! And you're here in Bayport?" Joe said eagerly. "What kind of story?"

Clayton Silvers threw up his hands and chuckled. "Now, wait a minute," he said. "I'm here on vacation."

"And you never called to say you were coming," Aunt Gertrude said, somewhat annoyed.

"I didn't even know you were still living here," Clayton Silvers explained. "Besides"—Silvers began brushing dust off his jacket—"you know Fenton was never one of my fans."

Frank and Joe exchanged curious glances. "Why not?" Frank asked.

"He felt I used to get his older sister in a lot of

trouble." Clayton Silvers smiled at Aunt Gertrude. "Had trouble getting him to believe it was the other way around."

"Oh, I want to hear *all* about this!" Joe said enthusiastically. "Why don't you come on by the house so we can—"

"I can't now," Clayton blurted out. He glanced at his watch, and once again Joe noticed the uneasiness in the man's manner. "I . . . I have an appointment in here," he said, indicating the mini mall. "An early dinner, but I'd be glad to stop by for a visit tomorrow."

"Fine then," Gertrude Hardy said. "Come for lunch, around one o'clock. All right?" She jotted their address on a slip of notepaper and handed it to Clayton.

"I'll be there. Now I really have to run, but I'll see you all tomorrow. Promise." Clayton Silvers took a few steps, then turned back to the Hardys. "Good to see you again, Spitfire!" He laughed, then hurried into the mini mall.

Gertrude Hardy appeared to be flustered as she started back toward the Hardys' van. "Let's go, boys. We still have to finish those errands."

The boys fell in behind her. "I think Silvers is here on a story," Joe whispered to Frank. "Did you notice how he clammed up when we asked questions?"

"He did seem a little jittery for a guy on vacation,"

Frank replied. "But I thought it was because of the mugging."

"That's another thing," Joe said. "Did you notice the clothes on those muggers? They were pretty well dressed for guys who make street grabs."

Frank nodded. "*Grab* is the word," he said. "The incident had a professional feel to it," he added. "Two for the pull, and a man at the wheel. I think they were trying to kidnap him."

Joe came to a sudden stop. "Stall Aunt Gertrude. I want to see who Mr. Silvers is meeting for that *early* dinner. Maybe that is part of the picture."

"But we have no right to—"

Joe was already running back down the street, and a few seconds later he had ducked through the main entrance to the mini mall.

The mall was a one-story building, about a block long and constructed in a C shape. Most of Joe's friends hung out at the large mall outside of town that contained lots of stores, arcades, a food court, and a multiplex movie theater. This mall specialized in novelties, bookstores, and a fancy coffeehouse.

Joe knew it did not have any major restaurants, so he wondered why Clayton Silvers was having a dinner date there. Moving quickly, Joe jogged by the stores from one end of the mall to the other. He stopped now and then when he spotted someone who looked like Mr. Silvers.

By the time he reached the far end of the mall, he

had not seen his quarry anywhere. Joe was about to run back to join Frank and his aunt when someone opened an exit door leading to the parking lot. The rectangle of bright light caught Joe's attention, and he got a glimpse of a man wearing a jacket the same style and color as Silvers's.

Joe ran to the door and pushed through it, spotting the man walking toward the far end of the parking lot. The lot was packed, giving Joe plenty of vehicles to hide behind as he followed his aunt's friend.

The setting sun cast a rich orange and red glow over everything—cars, trees, buildings, even people. Despite that, Joe could tell that the man Mr. Silvers was walking up to was pale as a ghost.

He was short and thin, with a flat nose and beady eyes that sparkled like those of a rat. Joe moved closer and ducked behind an old station wagon to watch as the man gave Silvers a leering smile. Joe could not see Silvers's face, but judging from his body language, Mr. Silvers was anxious, eager, or angry.

The little man made a gesture by rubbing his thumb and first two fingers together. Without hesitation, Clayton Silvers reached inside his jacket, withdrew a plain white envelope, and handed it to his companion.

The rat-eyed man grinned, and Joe couldn't help feeling he was about to bite Silvers's throat. The man handed Clayton Silvers a folded sheet of paper and then tore open the envelope. Joe watched as the reddish orange of the sunset washed over the crisp green bills in the ghostlike hand—hundred-dollar bills.

and Clayton Silvers. I told Joe, he said, "all
about my trip." He stopped. "Joe's right in part.
The reason for the story was to travel. Someday
soon I hope to take the trip I just described to
him."

3 Tips and Tales

This man is not a travel agent, Joe told himself. So
Clayton Silvers's vacation story was just that, a
story.

Silvers unfolded the sheet of paper the little man
had given him and read it carefully. Then he tore it
into pieces and dropped it into a Dumpster near
them. The two men continued talking for another
few minutes, and Joe could tell the little man was
very excited about something. As he talked, his arms
and hands flapped about like a marionette's.

Just as Joe had decided to get closer to eavesdrop
on their conversation, the two men split up and took
separate exits out of the parking lot. Clayton Silvers
headed back into the mall, the little man toward a
side street.

14

Joe let Silvers walk back into the shopping center before he stepped out of his hiding place and ran to the exit the little man had taken. The path led through an adjoining parking lot behind a bank, but the man was nowhere in sight.

Thinking quickly, Joe ran back to the Dumpster. Glancing around to make sure no one was watching, Joe leaned in, holding his breath against the odor of various decaying items. Joe spotted the torn bits of the note lying on top of a plastic garbage bag. He gingerly removed them and slipped them into the pocket of his windbreaker.

Within minutes Joe was approaching the Hardys' van with Frank and Aunt Gertrude sitting in the front seats.

"Where did you go?" Joe's aunt asked impatiently.

"I thought I left something in the store," Joe replied as he climbed into the passenger seat behind his aunt.

"Did you find it?" she asked.

"Yes," Joe said slyly. "I got . . . it."

"Good." Aunt Gertrude gave Frank the signal to start the vehicle. "We may not have time to finish the errands, but I have to pick up a few extra things for lunch tomorrow."

Joe leaned back in his seat and grinned. "That's right," he said. "Mr. Silvers will be there . . . ready to tell all, I hope."

Frank chuckled as he pulled away. Aunt Gertrude

studied a shopping list she had just written—a little too hard.

When the Hardys finally got home, the boys spent half an hour unloading the van and putting things away, while their aunt supervised and cooked.

Dinner consisted of a tender, juicy meat loaf with baby red bliss potatoes and buttered asparagus. The vegetable was one of Aunt Gertrude's favorites . . . just not everybody else's. Several times Joe wished they had a dog he could slip food to under the table.

Since their mother, Laura, was away visiting a relative, and their father, Fenton, was having dinner with a new client, the boys ate with their aunt, then went out to the backyard to talk. Joe was anxious to get Frank's take on what he had seen.

"So he met with this short guy, slipped him some money, then took off?" Frank repeated after Joe had brought him up to date.

"That's about the size of it," Joe replied.

"And you think you know the guy Mr. Silvers met?"

Joe shrugged. "I think I've seen him around town, but I can't be sure." He fished the slips of torn paper out of his pocket and laid them down on the picnic table.

After a few minutes of moving the pieces around, the boys found they had only part of the message. An upper corner and two pieces from the center were missing.

Joe frowned. "I missed a few pieces."

"We can read most of it," Frank said. "Looks like . . . 'target . . . worth millions . . . check out point man . . . three days left.' "

"So why'd Clayton tell us he was on vacation?" Joe asked.

"Probably he didn't want to worry Aunt Gertrude," Frank replied. "You know how she can be."

"I thought I did," Joe said, leaning back in his chair. "But after what she did today, and what Mr. Silvers hinted at . . . I'm not sure."

"I'm curious about what he said about Dad," Frank said. "That Dad didn't like him much. I want to talk to Dad about that."

"His new job is going to keep him pretty busy," Joe replied. "He didn't tell us who he's working for. Maybe he won't even be here when Clayton comes to lunch tomorrow."

Frank gathered up the pieces of the torn note. "Well, maybe we'll learn more tomorrow," he said.

"Especially about Spitfire," Joe said.

The boys laughed, then went back inside the house.

The next morning Frank and Joe weren't too upset about being stuck at home. The sky was steel gray, and a relentless drizzle spattered the windowpanes.

Frank tinkered around in the basement while Joe went back to bed.

It was eleven-thirty when Frank came up out of the basement to find his aunt rushing around the kitchen, preparing lunch. "I can't remember—what time is Mr. Silvers arriving?" he asked.

"We had said one, but when he called, I told him twelve-thirty would be good," Aunt Gertrude replied. She was placing slices of smoked turkey around a large oval platter. The edges of the meat were brown, with a slight sheen to them.

"Honey glazed?" Frank asked, licking his upper lip.

"Yes," Gertrude Hardy replied. "There's also ham, rye and pumpernickel breads, three types of cheese, pickles, and a German cole slaw."

Frank lounged against the doorframe. "We haven't had a lunch like this since you were working for the mayoral race. Who are you trying to impress now?"

"No one," Aunt Gertrude protested.

"You and Mr. Silvers never dated, did you?"

"No," Aunt Gertrude insisted. She stared at Frank, then smiled. "Clayton represents another time in my life . . . one I haven't thought about for a long while."

"What do you mean?" Frank asked. Before his aunt could answer, Fenton Hardy walked into the room. "When did you get back, Dad? You were gone when I woke up."

"Just a few minutes ago," Fenton Hardy replied.

He was a well-built man, strong, good looking, with brown hair and eyes. He wore a crisp white shirt, print tie, and a pair of light gray slacks. "I have to go back right after lunch."

"Can't you tell us what you're working on?" Frank asked.

"Not yet," his father replied as he reached for one of the cherry tomatoes that Aunt Gertrude was stacking in a serving bowl.

His sister lightly smacked his hand. "They're for lunch," she scolded. "If you'd had a decent breakfast instead of just a cup of coffee—"

"Yes, ma'am," Fenton teased. "You sound like Mother."

"Obviously the women of this family received all the common sense," Aunt Gertrude replied, without missing a beat.

Frank chuckled. "So, Dad, Mr. Silvers said you didn't like him."

Fenton Hardy raised an eyebrow. "That's not exactly true." Mr. Hardy took a container of orange juice from the refrigerator. "Even though Gertrude was older than I was, Dad expected me to look after her."

"And you jumped at the job," his sister replied. She turned to Frank. "Your father had detective instincts even when he was fourteen. Always checking on me and—"

"Only when Mom and Dad didn't know where you

were," Fenton interrupted. "In high school, Aunt Gertrude almost always came home late."

"Aunt Gertrude?"

All eyes turned to Joe Hardy as he stumbled into the kitchen, sleepy-eyed, barefoot, and wearing a wrinkled T-shirt and cutoff shorts. "Tell me more."

"I was involved in a lot of after-school programs," Gertrude Hardy replied huffily.

"You mean like the French club and stuff?" Joe asked.

"No," Fenton Hardy said. "More like human rights groups and community programs. My sister was even involved in a couple of mid-sixties protest rallies."

Both boys stared at their aunt in disbelief.

"Why does that shock you?" she asked indignantly.

"Uh . . ." was all Joe could say.

Frank did not do much better. "It's just that . . . well, uh . . ."

"I see." Aunt Gertrude appeared a little hurt by their reactions. "Clayton will be here in a little bit. I suggest you both wash up. Then you can help me set the table."

Gertrude Hardy began tearing leaves from a head of lettuce and rinsing them.

"Go on, boys," their father instructed. "We can talk more later."

By the time Clayton Silvers arrived, everything was ready. If there were any bad feelings between their father and Clayton Silvers, the boys could not detect them. Fenton Hardy had vigorously shaken Silvers's hand when he arrived, and they had been laughing and talking easily for the past half-hour during lunch.

Aunt Gertrude joined in and even mentioned some of the cases Fenton and the boys had worked on.

"And that was how we broke that smuggling case," Joe said, trying not to boast. "Dad got the big boss, and we caught the underlings."

"I think I remember reading about that," Mr. Silvers said. "Seems like you boys are following in your dad's footsteps."

"We want to," Frank replied, and glanced at his father, who seemed to be lost to the world, studying Clayton's face. Was something wrong? Frank wondered.

"Enough about us, Mr. Silvers," Joe insisted. "Tell us about *your* job."

For the first time since he arrived, Clayton Silvers appeared to be uncomfortable.

"You work for a major Washington newspaper, right?" Frank asked.

"I'm on vacation," Clayton replied, then took a sip of his after-lunch coffee. "I'd rather not talk shop now."

"We just wondered what paper," Joe went on.

"I used to work for the *Post*," Clayton replied.

"Now I'm freelance. I cover whatever I want for whichever paper will pay me." Clayton took another sip.

"Perhaps Clayton will tell us about his adventures another time, boys," Fenton Hardy cut in. "I know what it's like to try to leave things behind . . . especially tough things."

Frank noticed the look exchanged between the two men. What was going on? Was there a problem, or did their father know why Clayton had come to Bayport?

"Sure," Clayton said. "Another time. I'll be around for at least a week."

"Okay," Joe said. "Tell us about Aunt Gertrude when you guys were younger. Especially that nickname."

"Clayton—"

"Gertrude Hardy," Clayton interrupted, "you've got nothing to be ashamed of."

Aunt Gertrude rose from the table. "Well, I don't have to listen to you while you tell tales." There was a faint smile on her face as she began clearing the table.

Fenton Hardy offered to help, and the two of them carried dishes into the kitchen.

"Your aunt was a very willful person back then," Clayton began. "Full of ideals about right and wrong, and intensely opposed to injustice and prejudice."

"She really protested?" Frank asked eagerly.

"Sure," Clayton replied. "That's how we met, during a rally for better jobs and salaries for minorities."

"What about the nickname?" Joe asked.

Clayton chuckled. "A group of us had been protesting against some big-time Realtor who was trying to evict the tenants from a block of buildings in our neighborhood. He owned most of the tenement houses and had cut off the heat to them—trying to freeze the tenants out. We drew a lot of attention to them with our articles and protests. Then we started getting pressure to back off."

"You mean strong-arm stuff?" Frank asked.

"No," Clayton said. "Pressure from people who wanted the old tenements gone, and new businesses. Most kids backed off but not Spitfire. She and I kept it going. Flyers, letters, articles. They couldn't scare her, or me."

"Did you win?"

"No," Clayton replied. "But we gave them a good fight. In fact, our work got us both noticed. I got a scholarship to study journalism in college, and your aunt got one to study political science."

"Whoa!" Joe exclaimed. "Then I wonder why she never pursued a career in politics, or something."

Clayton rose from the table and glanced at his watch. "That's something she'd better answer herself." He glanced out the window, and his eyes narrowed.

"Something wrong, sir?" Frank asked, noting the change.

"Not at all," Clayton said. "I've just noticed the time. I need to do a couple of things, and since it's not raining so hard, now is a good time to go."

As Clayton went into the kitchen to say goodbye to Fenton and Aunt Gertrude, Joe stepped to the window.

"You saw it, too?" Frank asked, joining his brother.

"Yeah," Joe said.

A fine steady rain continued to fall. The street outside looked like polished black marble, and the leaves on the trees glistened.

Joe took only a moment to notice this before he spotted the white van parked half a block away.

"That looks like the van the muggers used yesterday," Joe said.

Frank nodded. "Same thing I thought. Muggers— or kidnappers."

"Muggers don't stalk the same victim for two days," Joe said. "Let's check them out."

The boys grabbed rain jackets off a rack by the front door and quietly slipped outside. They strolled to the sidewalk, appearing to be headed for their own van. Then, when they reached the curb, they turned and nonchalantly strolled toward the van.

"Let's just get close enough to see if the same guys are—"

Frank caught a glimpse of the interior of the van just before the engine roared to life—it was the same two men. The dark-skinned man was behind the wheel. The blond one was reaching for something in a white cardboard box on the dashboard.

"They're making a break for it!" Joe shouted as he ran into the street.

For a split second Joe felt excitement as he recognized the attackers, then the excitement was gone. Tires screeched as the van leaped forward. As the vehicle raced toward him, Joe realized that the driver was determined to make his getaway . . . even if it meant running him down.

Joe twisted, preparing to run, but his foot slipped on the slick, wet blacktop, and he fell, hard, right in the path of the oncoming van.

4 Hard Headlines

The Hardys jumped to their feet to give chase, but the van had disappeared around a corner before they could even reach their own van.

"Let's go after them," Joe insisted, grabbing for the door handle.

"No good," Frank replied, turning to his brother. "No keys. I left them in the house."

Joe smacked the van in frustration, then started back into the house.

"First he's attacked by two thugs," Joe grumbled. "Then he pays off a stoolie in a parking lot. Now the same thugs show up at our house, probably tailing him." He wiped the rain from his eyes. "I don't care what Mr. Silvers says, he's got to be after a story!"

"About dangerous people, obviously," Frank added as they reached the front door. "We'd better keep an eye on him as long as he's around Aunt Gertrude. Maybe we should—"

Frank stopped as he noticed an expensive two-door town car pull up in front of their driveway. A well-dressed man in a suit and raincoat stepped out of the car and started toward them.

"Excuse me," he said. "Is Fenton Hardy at home?"

"Yes," Frank replied. "Is he expecting you, Mr. . . . ?"

"Dean," the man replied. "Harlan Dean. I have an appointment."

"I'm Joe Hardy, and this is my brother, Frank." Joe extended his right hand. "Are you my dad's new client?"

Before the man could answer, the front door opened, and Fenton Hardy stood there smiling at the new arrival. "Come on in, Harlan," he said. "I see you've met my sons, my very wet sons," he added when he saw the boys' sopping-wet pants. When neither Frank nor Joe said anything about why they were wet, Fenton pointedly raised an eyebrow in their direction.

Mr. Dean nodded and walked in, followed by the boys.

"I'll be ready to leave in a minute," Fenton said. "Would you like some coffee?"

"No, thanks," Mr. Dean replied. He scanned the

room quickly, appearing to take in everything around him. "I'm anxious to get started."

"Then let me grab my coat, and we can go."

"Grab mine, too," Clayton Silvers said as he and Aunt Gertrude walked into the vestibule. "I have to go, also."

Fenton quickly introduced Mr. Dean to the others.

"Clayton Silvers," Mr. Dean said slowly. "Have we met?"

"I don't think so," Clayton replied as he reached for his raincoat.

"Clayton is a Washington reporter," Aunt Gertrude said.

"Maybe that's it," Mr. Dean replied. "I'm in Washington quite a lot."

"Guess that is it," Clayton said. "Sorry to eat and run—"

"You always did in the past," Aunt Gertrude teased. "Why should now be any different from then?"

"Boys, you can help your aunt with the dishes," Fenton said as he put on his trench coat.

"Not really, Dad," Joe protested. "We have to change, and then we're supposed to meet Iola and Callie in thirty minutes."

"That's plenty of time," Fenton said cheerfully. "Will we see you again while you're in town, Clayton?"

"Naturally," Clayton replied. "I'm on vacation. Besides, Gertrude has promised to show me around a bit. I'll call you in about an hour," he said to Aunt Gertrude.

Frank and Joe exchanged glances, then watched as Clayton Silvers drove off in his car. A few moments later their father and Mr. Dean slipped into Dean's car and drove away.

"Well, boys, go towel off, and then let's get to those dishes."

"Okay, Aunt Gertrude," Joe replied. "We'll be right there."

"We've got to figure out what Mr. Silvers is up to," Frank said when they were upstairs changing. "I'm worried because Aunt Gertrude is hanging out with him, and he has two guys stalking him."

"Let's go hang out with Iola and Callie," Joe said. "Then maybe we'll be able to figure out what to do next."

"Boys!" their aunt called from the kitchen.

Frank sighed heavily. "Okay," he replied. "Let's get those dishes done, or we'll be late."

Iola Morton and Callie Shaw had been dating Joe and Frank Hardy for a while. They were used to the boys chasing bad guys and solving crimes. Several times they had been right in the middle of an adventure and helped the Hardys. So they weren't surprised when the boys arrived fifteen minutes late to pick them up at Callie's house.

"Well, it's stopped raining at least," Callie told

Frank as she stepped out onto her front porch.

"Sorry," Frank said as he kissed Callie hello.

Iola slipped her arms around Joe's waist. "What took you so long?" she asked.

The boys were bringing them up to date on the day's events and were just at the part about spotting the white van, when one pulled up in front of Callie's house.

Instantly, Frank and Joe started pushing the girls back toward the front door.

"Get inside, quick!" Joe ordered.

"What for?" Iola insisted.

"That truck," Frank said.

Callie glanced at the van. "Oh, you mean the cable guys?"

As the van came to a stop, the Hardys noticed the words printed on the side.

"Stellar Dish Television," Frank said aloud.

"Problems with your cable?" Joe asked.

"No," Callie explained. "These guys sell the latest in radar dish TV service. They're new, their prices are low, and everybody's raving about them."

"Why were you guys so nervous about them?" Iola asked.

The service installer got out of the truck, and the boys could see he wasn't either of the men they had encountered.

"We'll explain on the way to the park," Frank said.

"You still want to play soccer?" Callie asked.

"Sure," Joe said. "Unless you're afraid you'll lose and want to forfeit the game."

Iola playfully punched Joe in the shoulder. "Not a chance, hot shot. Let's go."

By the time they reached the park, the Hardys had finished telling the girls about the white van and the thugs they'd fought.

"Do you guys have a sign over your house?" Iola teased. "Mysteries Are Us. No matter what, someone is always dropping a case in your laps."

Joe grinned devilishly. "It's tough being both a crime and a babe magnet."

Iola took a swing at his shoulder, but the younger Hardy hopped out of the way.

"Can you trust this Clayton Silvers?" Callie asked.

"Time will tell," Frank replied cheerfully. "For now, let's go play."

Though the ground was muddy, the foursome played soccer for half an hour and remained relatively clean. Then it started raining again.

"There goes the game," Frank said after they'd all piled into the van to get out of the wet.

"And we were winning," Iola teased.

"Tied," Joe insisted.

"Yeah, right." Iola playfully shook her head to spray Joe with the water from her hair.

"Anybody hungry?" Callie asked.

"Not after our lunch," Frank replied. "But I could go for something to drink."

"Let's go to Pizza Palace," Iola suggested.

"Great," said Joe. "But let's make a stop at the *Bayport Times* on the way."

"Why?" Frank asked.

"A guy in my world history class works there as an intern," Joe explained. "Maybe he can give us some information on another reporter. You girls mind?"

Callie and Iola answered in unison, "Do we ever?"

Frank pulled the van into the small parking lot of one of Bayport's major newspapers. The four slightly damp teenagers pushed through the glass doors and went up the staircase to the second-floor offices of the *Bayport Times*.

One long counter separated the entryway from the rest of the large, main room. There was one small private office on the right side of the room.

Six desks were set up around the main area, each covered with papers, letters, and computers. Four of the desks were occupied by someone either typing or talking on the phone. A line of four-drawer file cabinets ran along one wall, with books and newspapers piled on top.

There was a tall, sickly-looking green plant standing in front of the large window that overlooked the parking lot. It was the only decoration in the room. Everything else was practical and messy.

A thin teen with his long hair done up in braids walked over to the counter.

"Hey, Joe," he said cheerfully. "What brings you here?"

"Hey, Darryl," Joe said, giving him a high-five. "We came to pick your brain."

"For you, Frank, or the lovely ladies?" Darryl flashed a winning smile.

"Us," Joe replied dryly.

"Too bad," Darryl teased. "Seriously, you guys on to something?"

"Could be," Frank replied. "What do you know about a reporter named Clayton Silvers?"

"Take 'Em Down Silvers?" Darryl looked very excited. "I know the good and the bad."

"What do you mean?" Frank asked.

Darryl told them to wait a minute, then he ran over to one of the file cabinets. He extracted a folder and a few seconds later laid it open in front of the Hardys. The folder was filled with newspaper clippings, and all of them appeared to have been written by Clayton Silvers.

"I've followed his career for the past three years," Darryl said. "He was the best undercover, crime-stopping, conspiracy-busting reporter on the East Coast. The top dog!"

"So we've heard," Joe said.

"He brought down mobsters as well as crooked politicians and corporations. Nothing and nobody was too big for him." Darryl spread out a few of the clippings so the Hardys, Callie, and Iola could read the headlines. "I wanted to be just like him. He cost some powerful folks some serious green. Guess he made some, too."

Frank looked up from one of the clippings to see that Darryl had lost his enthusiasm. "What do you mean?"

Darryl pulled a clipping from the bottom of the pile and spread it out on the counter. The bold black type spelled out an unbelievable accusation. " 'Silvers Is Tarnished,' " Darryl quoted without looking at the paper. " 'Well-known reporter accused of taking bribes.' "

"Bribes for what?" Callie asked.

"They found proof he had this big Swiss bank account," Darryl replied sadly. "It contained more than a hundred thousand dollars he'd taken as payment to prove only *certain* people were dirty."

"You mean he lied in his articles?" Joe said.

"No," Darryl explained. "People paid him to go after their opponents or business rivals. They'd even given him tips and leads. He made their rivals look bad, so *his* clients looked good."

"This is too wild!" Joe Hardy exclaimed. "How are we going to tell Aunt Gertrude that her old, *best* friend . . . is a crook?"

5 Dangerous Curves

"You said they found proof of all this?" Frank Hardy asked Darryl.

The young newspaper intern shrugged. "They found enough evidence to accuse him, write the articles, and get him fired," Darryl said. "But not enough to go to court."

"Funny Dad didn't know about any of this," Frank said. "He's in and out of Washington on cases, and he has a lot of contacts there."

"Maybe he did know," Joe said. "I thought he gave Mr. Silvers a strange look when he wouldn't talk about his work."

"Are you going to tell your aunt?" Callie asked.

"I don't know," Frank replied. "We don't want to

hurt her. Besides, no one's *proved* he did these things."

"But what about the guys following him?" Joe asked once they were back in the van. "Mr. Silvers is into something here in Bayport, and it could get Aunt Gertrude hurt."

"So, let's find out what it is," Frank said evenly. "And the best way is to talk to Mr. Silvers face-to-face."

Joe smiled. "We go to his hotel?"

Frank nodded and put the van into gear. "As soon as we drop off Callie and Iola."

"Why can't we come with you?" Iola asked.

"We don't know him all that well," Frank explained. "It may be hard to get him to talk. But he sure won't talk if there's a crowd."

The girls shrugged with disappointment but finally agreed.

"One of these days," Iola said, "we'll tackle our own mystery. Then we'll be leaving you guys behind."

"Sherlock Shaw and Morton, P.I." Joe grinned devilishly. "I like it."

The four of them burst out laughing as Frank drove them through the puddled streets of Bayport.

It was three-thirty by the time Frank and Joe pulled up in front of the Bayport Plaza Hotel. The hotel was one of the best in town. All red brick, white trim, and large windows, the six-story building sat on a hill in the center of town, surrounded by upscale stores and restaurants. The lobby had Persian rugs and waxed oak floors, with white marble pillars and crystal chandeliers.

"What room did he say he was in?" Joe asked as they approached the front desk.

"Five-fifteen, I think," Frank replied.

"We'd like to see Mr. Silvers," Joe told the clerk. "He's in—"

"No, he's not," the man replied matter-of-factly.

Joe leaned forward. "Excuse me?"

"Mr. Silvers is not in." The man adjusted his wire-rimmed glasses and stared at the boys with a bored expression. The brass tag on his maroon jacket read, Albert Tally, Assistant Manager. "Would you like to leave a message?"

"How do you know he's not in?" Frank asked patiently.

"Because he went out a little while ago. Would you like to—"

"Do you know where he—"

"No," Mr. Tally said dryly. "Would you—"

"It's really important that we—"

"I'm sure it is," the assistant manager said, interrupting Joe for the second time. "But I cannot give you any information. Would you like to leave a message?"

"That's too bad," Frank said. "He was waiting for some important information from our father."

"And who would that be?" Mr. Tally asked in a dry tone.

"Fenton Hardy," Frank replied. "We'll just have to tell Dad—"

The eyes behind the gold-rim glasses lit up. "You're Mr. Hardy's sons?"

"Yes," Joe said. "I'm Joe, he's Frank."

"I am *so* sorry," the assistant manager said with more energy. "I didn't realize this was business-related. I've only been here a short while, but I hear your father has done this hotel a world of good in the past. Saved us from a most embarrassing situation. And now . . . well, we don't need to talk about that, do we?"

Joe looked puzzled. "No, I guess we don't."

"Mr. Silvers left about thirty minutes ago with a friend," the assistant manager said.

"Did you see this *friend?*" Joe asked with some annoyance.

"Oh, yes." Mr. Tally glanced around suspiciously, then leaned in closer to the boys. "I've been keeping an eye on his comings and goings. Low profile, of course. She was middle-aged with light brown hair," Mr. Tally said. "The friend was wearing cream-colored slacks with a matching blouse and a cocoa-colored jacket."

"Aunt Gertrude!" Joe exclaimed.

"Oh really?" the assistant manager mused. "Is Mr. Silvers a suspect in—"

"No," Frank interrupted. "He's working on a case with our dad."

"Oh . . ." The assistant manager looked puzzled. "Your father didn't mention that earlier when he told me—"

"Our dad was here?" Joe asked.

"Just for a little while, but he—"

"You don't know where Mr. Silvers went, do you?" Frank cut in.

"No, but he asked about the view from the Bayport Sounds area, then drove off in his friend's car."

"Thanks," Frank said. "Come on, Joe."

"I wonder why Dad came to see Mr. Silvers," Joe said as they jumped into the van.

"Maybe he wanted to ask him about that mess in Washington," Frank speculated. "Maybe he thought he could help clear him."

"Could be," Joe said, but he was not convinced.

Frank drove along the main street for several blocks, then turned left and took the road that led east toward the shore. Bayport Sounds was a two-mile collection of beach and small houses that commanded a great view of the bay. Only a few of them were inhabited year-round. Most were summer homes or vacation rentals.

"If Mr. Silvers is staying at the hotel, why would he come out this way?" Joe asked after about ten minutes of silence.

"There's a cliffside view that attracts a lot of tourists during the summer," Frank replied. "Remember, Aunt Gertrude wanted to show him

around. That would be a place to start. Keep an eye out for Aunt Gertrude's car."

Just then a Land Rover came roaring down the highway, going in the opposite direction. As the vehicle passed them, Frank noticed a white cardboard box of doughnuts on the dashboard and, behind the wheel, the dark-skinned assailant.

"That was the guy in the van who nearly ran you over earlier!" Frank exclaimed. "And it looked like the other guy was with him."

Joe twisted around to catch a glimpse of the departing vehicle. He could just make out the first three digits of the license plate before it was out of sight. "Six five three was all I could get," he told Frank. "Should we go after them?"

"No," Frank replied. "They're going too fast, and by the time we turn around they'll be gone."

"You're right," Joe agreed. "Let's hope they didn't find Silvers and Aunt Gertrude already."

The boys rode silently for several more minutes, hoping they wouldn't find that their aunt and her friend had been in the Land Rover, victims of the two attackers.

Just as Frank was ready to turn around and head back to town, Joe called out, "There it is!" He was pointing to Aunt Gertrude's midsize car sitting in a parking lot near a cliffside lookout.

Frank pulled into the parking area and brought the van to a halt next to the car. There were no other cars in the small lot, but there was no sign of their aunt or Silvers, either.

A narrow winding path led up a sandy incline to the top of the cliff. Waist-high grass and shrubs, pale and thick, bordered both sides of the pathway. Frank and Joe ran up the hill, glancing from side to side for any signs of danger or a struggle. Had the thugs already found their aunt and Clayton Silvers? Had they harmed her in an attempt to kidnap Clayton? All this and other frightening images hammered at them until they reached the plateau.

Their aunt and Clayton Silvers stood about fifteen feet ahead of them, staring out over a long stretch of beach and some of the homes below. Frank and Joe breathed a sigh of relief. Everything looked fine, until they started toward the couple. Then they noticed that Clayton was scanning the area with more than a tourist's interest. He had a pair of high-powered binoculars in his hands.

"I've got to locate them, but they could be any-where," the boys heard him say. "Normal and harm-less looking, until it's too late."

"Until what's too late?" Frank asked.

Aunt Gertrude jumped from fright and grabbed Clayton's arm. She released a deep sigh when she saw the boys. "My goodness, you scared the life out of me," she scolded. "Don't ever do that again."

The boys offered their apologies.

"Why are you boys up here?" she asked. "Did you come up with Callie and Iola?"

"We were just driving around," Joe replied, attempting nonchalance. "We spotted your car and decided to come say hello."

Gertrude Hardy studied her nephew for a few seconds, then glanced at Clayton. "They're just like their father," she told him. "They never could lie to me." She turned back to the boys. "Did you think I needed a chaperon?"

"No," Joe protested. "We're just—"

"Don't bother, Joe," Frank told his younger brother. "Mr. Silvers will find out that we stopped by his hotel, looking for him."

Clayton Silvers frowned.

"A few things have happened today," Frank continued. "And we felt . . . we needed to talk to you."

The boys told their aunt and her friend about spotting the van outside their house, how it had nearly run them down, and what they learned at the newspaper.

Joe turned to their aunt. "We didn't want you to learn about any of this before we talked to him."

"I knew about it," Aunt Gertrude said calmly.

"You did?" Joe exclaimed. "But—"

"You must really think me an awful dullard," she told them. A cold, damp wind blew in off the water. Aunt Gertrude pulled her jacket tighter around her. "Can we have this discussion in the car?" she asked.

Joe and Frank nodded, then led the way back down the trail to the parking lot.

"When did you learn about this?" Frank asked, after they were all seated in Aunt Gertrude's car. She had started the car and turned on the heater.

"I read about it in the papers some time ago," Aunt Gertrude replied. "I tried to call Clayton when it happened, but he had already been fired and I didn't have his home number."

Clayton Silvers turned to the boys, who were sitting in the backseat. "Your aunt and I hadn't talked to each other for years," he explained. "We weren't angry or anything like that. It was just—"

"He became so full of himself," Aunt Gertrude interrupted. "After he started working as a reporter, he lost contact with his old friends."

Silvers chuckled. "You won't let me forget that, will you?" he said, shaking his head.

"No," Gertrude Hardy replied. "Then showing up here and pretending that nothing had happened. Really."

"What brought you to Bayport, Mr. Silvers?" Frank asked. "What are you looking for?"

"Not *what*," Clayton corrected. "*Who.*" He turned to Gertrude Hardy. "Can we drive around a little while I explain?"

Gertrude pulled out of the parking lot and continued up the main road toward the top of the cliff.

"The first conspiracy I uncovered lit up Washington and my career," Silvers said proudly. "I got a raise, respect, and a few threats." He smiled as if recalling some favorite memory. "But I didn't care. I had the bug. I knew what I wanted to do."

He continued his story slowly, being sure to explain every detail as if his life depended on it. Much of it was what the boys had already learned. But as they reached the top of the steep cliff and started down the other side, his story took on a new angle.

"I never took those bribes," he insisted. "I only went after those people because they were crooked—for no other reason."

"Then how do you explain the money in the Swiss bank account?" Frank asked.

"At first I couldn't," Silvers replied. "Because I didn't know who had framed me. I've made a few enemies in my time."

"You almost made another one," Aunt Gertrude said, shaking her head. "Telling me you were here on vacation." Suddenly the car swerved slightly toward the cliffside. Gertrude Hardy quickly straightened it again.

"Better keep your mind on the road, and not on teasing me, Spitfire," Clayton told her.

Frank and Joe chuckled until they noticed the car was picking up speed and swerving.

"Something's wrong!" Aunt Gertrude cried. There was fear in her voice as she struggled with the steering.

"Maybe we'd better pull over and stop," Clayton suggested.

"I'm trying to, but the brakes aren't holding."

The sedan weaved back and forth as it picked up more and more speed despite Aunt Gertrude's best efforts.

"Pump the brakes!" Joe shouted. He wanted to reach over the front seat and grab the wheel, but he was afraid that would make matters worse.

"I am!" Aunt Gertrude exclaimed. "But it's not working!"

Joe saw only the low metal guardrail and a hundred-foot drop to the beach below. Frank saw the oncoming traffic lane and the sharp protruding rocks of the cliff face. The boys couldn't choose which would be worse to steer toward. But as the car took another mad swerve toward the cliff face, the Hardys had the sickening feeling a choice was about to be made for them.

6 Nowhere to Go but Down

Joe could see the terror in his aunt's eyes reflected in the rearview mirror. Her fingers were gripping the steering wheel so tightly that the knuckles had turned white.

Sitting directly behind Aunt Gertrude, Frank Hardy saw the side of the cliff rushing toward them. They were in the oncoming lane now, whipping around a turn, and there was no way of knowing if another car or truck was bearing down on them.

Again, Aunt Gertrude twisted the wheel slightly. That single movement sent the car back into the proper lane, but now they were only inches from the cliff edge. Clayton Silvers and Joe Hardy both sucked in air as the rear wheel skidded on gravel and sand along the shoulder before Gertrude Hardy managed to get the car back on the road.

"You can do this, Aunt Gertrude," Frank said firmly, and gently placed his hands on her shoulders.

"But the brakes won't hold!" The words practically caught in her throat.

"I know," Frank said, and he did know from experience. He and Joe had been in this situation more times than he cared to remember. He knew one other thing: the longer this lasted, the sooner their luck would run out.

"Get into the left lane," he told his aunt.

"But the oncoming traffic!"

The road was straight now, and Frank could see the left lane was clear for a hundred feet or so. "We have to take the chance before we reach that next sharp turn!" he insisted.

"Side drag?" Joe asked, realizing what his brother was going for.

Frank nodded without looking at Joe and without taking his hands off his aunt's shoulders.

"We have to try to slow the car down by dragging it against something," he explained to her.

"The cliff?" Aunt Gertrude could not believe what he was asking her to do.

"Well, that's better than the option on this side," Clayton added, trying to sound flip. His voice trembled.

Gertrude Hardy turned the wheel, and the car

jerked left into the oncoming lane. She squeezed the steering wheel tighter as the tires slipped off the paved surface and onto grass and dirt. In an instant the sedan's metal body seemed to scream as it dragged against the sharp rock. The car jumped to the right from the impact, and Aunt Gertrude almost lost control of it.

They were in the right lane now. As they reached the turn, tires screeching, they all held their breath and Clayton made a grab for the steering wheel.

"Don't you dare!" Aunt Gertrude shouted. She steered the car away from the far edge and into the left lane and the turn. A Jeep went by with four teenagers in it. The two cars missed each other by scant inches.

"Oh my," Gertrude Hardy gasped. "I almost—"

"But you didn't," Joe interrupted.

Frank looked down the hill. Again it was clear for a few hundred feet before the next turn. "Do it again," he urged his aunt.

"Go for it, Spitfire," Clayton said. He was staring straight ahead, his left hand braced against the dashboard, his right hand gripping the door handle.

Aunt Gertrude didn't say a word. She didn't take her eyes off the road. Once more she steered the vehicle against the rocks. Again, it almost bounced back onto the road, but she held it as steady as she could.

There was the thud and the terrible screech of

metal. But they could feel the car slowing, just a little. Frank tried not to squeeze his aunt too tightly. He was prepared to lunge forward and grab the wheel if he had to, and he knew Joe would do the same. But their best chance for survival was if their aunt could bring them to a stop.

Another curve was coming up.

Again Aunt Gertrude steered the car toward the cliff face, desperately fighting to keep control. The tires kicked up more gravel and grass, and Aunt Gertrude knew the car would hit any second. Her grip on the wheel became tighter and tighter.

Something caught the front fender, and the car spun slightly to the left and smashed into the rocks, crushing the headlight and grille. Aunt Gertrude screamed as the car bounced back out onto the road, skidding toward the cliff edge.

Frank and Joe were thrown sideways against each other. Clayton Silvers's car door swung open, and his body could have been flung out of the vehicle, but his seat belt held.

Gertrude Hardy screamed as the car spun again and again, slowing it down. For a brief second, she had no sense of direction. She only felt an arm shoot past her and then something thump inside the steering column. There was a horrible grinding sound, and something seemed to tear in the engine. All at once the car came to a stop, and there was silence.

Joe was the first one out of the car. "We gotta move fast," he yelled as he helped Clayton Silvers out of the vehicle. The reporter's seat belt was jammed, so he had to slide out from under it. "We're across the road, and something could come around that curve and nail us!"

Frank was helping Aunt Gertrude. "Are you hurt?" he asked.

His aunt's eyes were wide, her mouth half opened in a funny O shape. She reluctantly let go of the wheel and allowed Frank to help her from the car.

The boys walked Clayton and Aunt Gertrude to the far side of the road, then they ran back to the vehicle.

"Let's push it to the side of the road before someone comes around that turn," Frank said. Working as quickly as they could, the boys managed to push the mangled vehicle into a slight ditch on the cliff side of the road. Joe quickly took a highway emergency pack out of the trunk and began setting up hazard flares every few feet.

By the time he rejoined Frank and the others, his aunt was more talkative. Gertrude Hardy was seated on a small white boulder, Clayton on the ground beside her.

"I've never had a problem with that car, especially the brakes," Gertrude Hardy said. She turned toward the boys slowly. "You know how often I take it to be serviced?"

Frank grinned weakly. "The garage mechanic is thinking of giving her frequent *service* miles," he teased. "Would you stay with her while we check out the car?" Frank asked Clayton. The reporter nodded but said nothing.

Joe pulled his cell phone from a holder on his belt. "Maybe you can call for a tow truck while you wait," he suggested. Both Clayton and his aunt nodded.

For fifteen minutes the boys checked under the hood and the underside of the car. They examined the steering column, the brake pads and drums. By the time they finished, they had a pretty good idea of what had happened.

"What did you find?" Aunt Gertrude asked them.

Frank hesitated. "Well, the car is pretty banged up," he said. "It's hard to be sure."

"Do not patronize me, Frank Hardy," Aunt Gertrude said sternly. "I am not a child, any more than you are."

Joe shrugged. "It looks like someone tampered with the brakes. The brake fluid lines were cut." Before he could say more Frank shot him a look to be quiet.

Clayton Silvers paced angrily. "They were after me," he said to Gertrude, "and that almost got you killed."

"*Why* is someone after you, sir?" Frank asked.

"Tell them, Clayton," Aunt Gertrude said. "They have a right to know."

"A little over a year ago, I was after some industrial thieves," he said. "These guys were the best of the best. There wasn't a laboratory or computer corporation that they couldn't get into. They hit places all over the United States."

"Those places have top security precautions," Frank said. "Guard patrols, pressure floors, video cameras, infrared lights, retina-scan code keys, and more."

"Yeah," Joe said. "We've gone up against some stuff like that. There's a plant around here, Fairmont Industries, that has that kind of security. We helped them out once."

"So how did these guys pull off the thefts?" Frank asked.

"That's what I wanted to find out," Clayton replied. "Especially since I was getting tips that these guys were moving up. I heard they were planning to go after weapons plans and government secrets."

"Are these guys spies?" Frank asked.

"No. Just thieves," Clayton replied. "But the worst kind. They'll sell anything to the highest bidder. No conscience. No loyalties."

"Tell them about your other concern, Clayton," Aunt Gertrude said.

Clayton Silvers rubbed his face and neck, then sighed heavily. "I'd started to pick up information that suggested these guys were connected to somebody big in Washington."

Joe's face lit up. "You mean, someone in the government, like the CIA or NSA?"

"I don't know if it's that high," Clayton replied. "But considering what they can do, and the kind of equipment they have access to . . . I don't know."

"Just as Clayton was starting to get close to these people," Aunt Gertrude said, "he was accused of those awful things."

"The money showed up in a Swiss bank account I'd never seen before," Clayton explained. "There was even an electronic trail that suggested I had made the deposits myself. Then there were records of purchases I had never made, expensive stuff. It just got worse and worse."

"Clayton couldn't prove his innocence, so he was fired," Aunt Gertrude said.

"Sometimes the media can work against a man," Clayton said. "A few of the very reporters I'd known for years were scrambling to get the goods on me. Friends!"

Joe exchanged a nervous glance with Frank, then turned to his aunt. "You agreed to help Mr. Silvers look for these guys?" he asked awkwardly.

Aunt Gertrude could tell her nephew was holding something back. "Yes," she explained. "Clayton said there were indications that these people set themselves up in the area near the place they plan to rob. There were unconfirmed rumors they were moving into Bayport, and obviously they're here and onto him. I thought I could help him look around where there is rental property." Abruptly she stopped. "But that's not what you're really asking, is it?" she concluded.

Joe and Frank didn't know what to say, but their aunt understood their silence.

"Yes, I believe Clayton is innocent," she replied. "Not just because he is a friend. Clayton has always thought well of himself. He has always been very proud of his accomplishments and achievements. He would never do anything to tarnish his reputation. Never."

Clayton smiled. "Are you trying to say I have a big ego?"

Aunt Gertrude chuckled. "Trying?"

The tow truck pulled up, and after Frank explained what had happened, the driver started hitching the damaged vehicle to his truck. He told the Hardys he'd give them a lift back to their van.

"I'll go with your aunt to the garage and make sure she gets home all right," Clayton said. "It's the least I can do. Then I'd suggest you all stay clear of me until—"

"As my nephews might say—I don't think so," Gertrude Hardy said. "I believe you're innocent, Clayton, and I will do what I can to help prove it."

"But—"

"We all will," Joe added.

"I'm sure our dad will help, too, once he hears what's happening," Frank offered.

"But I can't ask you to—" Silvers started to say.

"You haven't," Aunt Gertrude replied. "And you should know better than to try to talk me out of anything. From this point on, these thieves will have to deal with Hardys."

7 Tall Stories

"Then it's settled," Joe told his aunt. "How about we work on tracking down the thugs, while you and Mr. Silvers try to locate any newcomers to town."

"There's no way I can talk you people out of this?" Clayton Silvers asked. "You know what I'm up against. The danger and all."

"We'd keep digging on our own anyway," Joe replied.

Clayton Silvers shook his head. "This is exactly why I'm not married," he said softly. "I never wanted to put anyone I cared about in danger."

"Good thing our father didn't think the way you do," Joe replied.

"Our mom knew what she was getting into when she married a police officer," Frank added.

Clayton stared at the damaged car, then glanced over at Gertrude Hardy. "Sometimes life isn't that simple or kind."

Frank and Joe saw the look that passed between their aunt and Mr. Silvers.

"Okay," Clayton said reluctantly. "I'll accept your help. I've got this local stoolie who might know something," he continued. "He's been useful but expensive."

Frank realized Clayton was probably talking about the man Joe had seen him meet the day before in the mall parking lot.

"Then let's get going," Joe insisted, and they all squeezed into the tow truck and started up the hill to the Hardys' van.

"You two know how I feel about your getting into dangerous situations," Aunt Gertrude warned. "I was thinking we'd call your—"

"We'll be careful," Joe said. He gave his aunt a big smile. "Besides, it looks like sleuthing runs in the family."

"And all we plan to do is gather information," Frank assured her. "That's all."

"Well . . . all right." Reluctantly, Gertrude Hardy watched the boys climb out of the truck and walk over to their van as the tow truck pulled out of the lot.

"Why didn't you want me to tell them what else we found?" Joe asked as Frank popped the hood. "Don't you think they have a right to know? Especially Mr. Silvers."

"Sure he does," Frank replied. "But I want to be able to give him some answers, not more things to worry about." He reached into his shirt pocket and pulled out a small disk-shaped object. It was black, thin as a quarter, with two tiny wires dangling from one side. "Someone planted this tracking device on Aunt Gertrude's car," Frank continued. "That means they could have done the same with this van."

"Or sabotaged it." Joe dropped down to the ground and began examining the underside of the vehicle.

"I don't think it's likely, but it won't hurt to check it out," Frank said. "Then let's get into town and look for some answers."

The boys did not find any devices attached to their van, and ten minutes later they were back in Bayport.

On the way in, Joe had called their friend Tony Prito and told him about the case. Tony agreed to help them, so Frank drove straight to Tony's house.

"So you'll take the tracking device to Phil Cohen," Joe said to Frank as they pulled into the Pritos' driveway. Phil was another of the Hardys' closest friends, and a wizard with computers and electronics. "While Tony and I run around looking for the white van these thugs have been driving. Right?"

"Right," Frank replied. "Then we meet back at the

house and compare notes at supper. Aunt Gertrude said we wouldn't be eating until seven-thirty or eight, after the day she's had."

"Hey, guys," Tony said as he ran up to the van. "I've only got an hour before I have to be at work for the supper crowd, so let's do this."

"Sure thing," Joe said. He and Frank told Tony what they were looking for, and why.

"So you want me to drive you around looking for this van?" Tony asked when they were finished.

"Yeah," Joe replied. "We figured you know most of the garages and car repair shops around here. If these guys rented the van or had it serviced, or—"

"Or buy their gas at the same place," Tony interrupted. "Someone might know where they're staying."

"Exactly," Frank said. "Meanwhile, I'm going to check back with Darryl at the newspaper office—I hope he'll still be there—then head over to Phil Cohen's."

"Okay," Tony said cheerfully. "Let's do it."

Ten minutes later, as the sun began to set, Frank drove away from the Pritos' house in one direction, while Joe and Tony headed off in the other.

When they reached the street where the men had first attacked Clayton Silvers, Joe suggested they drive in an ever-widening spiral, checking every gas station and garage they could find. For a half-hour they talked to station attendants and cashiers, giving a description of the van and the men. After questioning a dozen people, they had nothing to show for it.

"Well, this is a bust," Joe grumbled as they pulled over by a phone booth.

"Except for that one guy at the last station," Tony reminded him.

Joe shrugged. "Yeah, but it turns out the van he saw belongs to that new cable TV company, Stellar Dish."

"The van was the same make and model," Tony insisted. "Maybe the thieves are using that company as their cover."

"Frank and I saw one of Stellar Dish's vans earlier today," Joe explained. "The company name is painted on the sides, clear as day."

"They could be using a truck they haven't labeled yet."

Joe didn't respond. He knew Tony could be right. The thieves could be using the company as cover. But it seemed stupid. Why use a van that could be spotted so easily and traced back to your base of operations? For that matter, why draw attention to yourself by trying to kidnap, then rub out someone in broad daylight? Surely the thieves knew that would bring the police into the picture, and possibly alert everyone to their operations, Joe told himself. Then he thought, Clayton had insisted on keeping the police out of it. Was that to make it easier for him to find the bad guys, or was he covering up something else? Whatever the answer, Joe told himself, Aunt Gertrude was in the middle of it, and he had to make sure she was safe.

"I said, I have to get to work soon." Tony's voice cut into Joe's thoughts. "You want me to drop you somewhere?"

"I'm sorry, Tony," Joe said. "I was thinking." Joe glanced out the front window and spotted the Bayport Plaza Hotel across the street. "You can let me out here," he said. "I'll call home to see how things are, then I might look around some more."

"Okay," Tony said as Joe climbed down from the pickup truck. "Maybe I can help you out again tomorrow. Give me a call."

Joe promised he would, then waved as Tony drove away. He moved to a phone booth and dialed his home number, all the time staring at the hotel.

Aunt Gertrude picked up the receiver on the first ring.

"Hey there," Joe said. "I just wanted to know how things are going."

"Not very well," Aunt Gertrude replied. "I've called around town, to the community center, and to a friend of mine who sells real estate locally. Nothing yet."

"I haven't had any luck either," Joe admitted. "Have you heard from Frank?" he asked.

"No," his aunt replied. "But Clayton said his, uh . . . *stoolie* believes something is *going down,* in

61

the next day or two. There are rumors floating through the underworld."

Joe chuckled silently. Hearing his aunt trying to use the lingo was pretty amusing, despite the seriousness of the situation.

"I want to call your father about all of this," Aunt Gertrude said. "But he's very busy with his latest case."

As Joe listened to his aunt, he stared up at the hotel building. He knew Clayton Silvers's room overlooked the main street, and he spotted his windows on the fifth floor. The shades were drawn, and the room appeared to be dark.

"You really trust Mr. Silvers, don't you?" Joe asked.

"Yes," his aunt replied. "Although I do believe there is something he's not telling me about all of this."

"Like what?" Joe asked.

"I don't know," his aunt replied. "But I'm trying to get it out of him now."

Just then the lights went on in Clayton's room.

"You're talking to him on the phone?" Joe asked. "Is he on the other line?"

"No," Aunt Gertrude replied. "Clayton is here at the house."

Joe froze. If Clayton Silvers was with his aunt, who had just turned on the lights in his room? "Aunt Gertrude, I have to go. If Frank calls in, tell him to meet me at . . . uh . . . " Joe glanced around quickly.

He didn't want his aunt asking a lot of questions or worrying. He spotted a bookstore down the block and gave her its name and address.

"All right," his aunt replied over the phone.

"Good," Joe said. "I'll talk to you later."

He quickly hung up and took one more look up at Clayton's window. The light was still on, and a shadow passed over the shade.

Joe hustled across the street, through the lobby, and into an elevator before anyone at the front desk spotted him. The elevator deposited him on the fifth floor, and Joe was thankful for the relative quiet with which the doors opened and closed.

The hallway was empty, and once Joe got his bearings, he moved swiftly down the corridor to Clayton's room. The door was metal with a brass lever door handle and a security card lock. If it was locked, Joe told himself, he'd have to wait for whoever was inside to come out.

But the door was not closed completely.

Once again, Joe glanced up and down the carpeted corridor. No one was in sight. He'd feel stupid if one of the crooks crept up on him while he was attempting to do the same to one of them. Joe slowly eased the door open, expecting to find someone going through Clayton's things.

The room was empty but trashed. Most of Clayton's belongings were spilled out in the middle of the floor.

Joe eased into the room, leaving the door wide open. The bathroom was to his right, the door open, the lights off. Joe glanced inside to see if anyone was hiding in the shower. But the shower curtain was wide open.

There was a closet on his left with a sliding door. Again Joe cautiously slid back the door, ready to move if someone sprang at him. Nothing. Perhaps whoever had ransacked the room had found what he wanted and taken off.

When Joe turned back to face the main room, everything went dark. Someone strong and fast had thrown a pillowcase over his head and was trying to wrestle him to the floor. Joe struck out at the assailant, landing a hard right to the man's ribs. He heard a grunt but was instantly slammed against a wall. Joe heard a door slam and realized he was still inside the room—now with the door closed. But he couldn't tell exactly where he was.

The attacker kept the pillowcase over Joe's head with one hand while trying to twist Joe's arm behind his back with the other. The two wrestled and stumbled around the room. Joe tried to break free of the man's grip, or at least to see who his attacker was. The man suddenly changed his tactics. He looped an arm around Joe's throat, effectively keeping the pillowcase in place, while strangling his victim.

Joe could barely breathe. He knew he had to break free before he passed out.

Joe violently twisted his body left, then right, as hard and as fast as he could. At the same time, he brought his right arm up, breaking the assailant's grip on his throat. The combined movements threw his attacker off balance for a moment.

Crouching low, Joe reached up to pull the case from his face. That was when the man moved to the front of Joe and raised his knee into Joe's chest. Joe flew backward, fully expecting to land on the floor or some piece of furniture. But a sudden impact, followed by the sound of shattering glass and a rush of air, told Joe where he was falling.

He grabbed blindly for anything he could seize. He was four stories up, and he didn't have to see to know what waited for him far below.

8 Big Brother Is Watching

Joe Hardy's hands shot out as he felt the rush of air and space around him. The wind stripped the pillowcase from his face, and his stomach twisted violently as the sickening sense of falling filled him with pure terror.

All the sensations overlapped and happened in a flash. The buildings were up and down and lying on their sides, all at the same time. He caught a quick glimpse of people looking up and shards of glass falling around him like raindrops.

Nothing was real, except his fear—until the fingers of his right hand felt rough stone. The windowsill, Joe's mind screamed in recognition. Instantly he clenched his hand into a clawlike grip. His body dropping through space arced in toward the building, until it slammed into the brick wall. The red bricks dug into his chest, ribs, and knees. Pain exploded throughout his body.

The air rushed out of his lungs, and his body swung and twisted wildly. Sharp bits of stone tore into Joe's fingertips as he held on for dear life. The street was four stories below, and Joe knew the fall would kill him.

As he bounced against the building again, Joe reached out with his left hand, grasping for another handhold. His fingers clawed frantically until they clamped onto the narrow lip of a large protruding brick. Joe held on with both hands, the windowsill with his right, the brick facing with his left.

Joe quickly jammed his foot into the pointing between two other bricks. The footing was precarious—not more than a quarter of an inch on which to rest some of his weight. But it held.

"Don't stop," Joe muttered out loud. "Climb." He knew either of his grips might give out at any moment. He took a deep breath and pushed up with his foot, while pulling up with both hands. Joe rose a few inches—just enough to reach up with his left hand and grab the windowsill.

Straining hard and ignoring his pain, Joe pulled himself up and over the windowsill, then tumbled into the room.

The room was dark, cool, and very empty.

He lay there on the rough carpeting, his breath

coming in short, raspy gulps. He felt the pain in his shoulder and side, and the stinging and burning where his flesh had been scraped or torn.

Slowly rising up onto his elbows, Joe looked around. Clayton Silvers's room had been searched by a pro. The dresser drawers were open and the contents thrown all over the floor.

His suitcase was open, but the few things in it— business folders, magazines—were still intact.

Whoever had been searching the room hadn't had time to finish the job. Joe's entrance must have interrupted him.

Joe turned on a lamp by the head of the bed. He examined his hands carefully. The skin on his fingers was scraped a bit, but all in all, he was fine. The next day the bruising would show.

He glanced about the room one more time, and something caught his attention. A thin plastic card was lying on the floor by the window. At first Joe thought it must be one of Clayton Silvers's credit cards, but when he picked it up, he saw the familiar magnetic strip on one side, but the other side was blank. A long strip of flexible plastic dangled from the card, like the tail of a kite.

What was it? Joe wondered.

The sounds of running feet caused him to turn toward the door. He managed to slip the card into his pocket just as Assistant Manager Tally opened the door and entered. Two men in dark blue blazers followed closely behind him. *Security* was stitched across their left breast pockets in yellow and red thread.

"What's going on here?" Alfred Tally shouted when he saw the room. He stared at Joe for a moment and became even more confused. "You're one of Mr. Hardy's sons! Why were you hanging out of the window?"

Joe's mind was racing. What should he say? Tell all, and bring down more attention on Clayton? That might scare off the techno thieves and ruin any chance of clearing Clayton's name.

Before Joe could think of a third option, things became more complicated. Fenton Hardy walked through the door, followed by his client, Harlan Dean. Both men appeared to be very tense and alert, taking in everything in a glance.

"Joe, what's going on here?" Fenton asked.

Joe grabbed at the first excuse that came to mind. "I came here to see Mr. Silvers and found a thief going through his stuff."

The assistant manager's eyes grew wide. His mouth opened and closed without a sound.

"We fought," Joe continued. "But he got away."

Fenton stepped up to Joe. He noticed the scratches on his hands. "And the broken window?" he asked.

"He threw me out, but I grabbed the windowsill." Joe explained how he'd survived the near-fatal en-

69

counter. The whole time, the assistant manager stood stiff as a board, with a look of horror on his face. One security man examined the room, while the other called in the incident on his two-way radio.

"I was just about to call the front desk when you arrived," Joe concluded.

"Whoever did this was thorough," Harlan Dean said. He was standing by the window staring at the sill and the broken glass. "And you were lucky," he told Joe.

"Guess so," Joe replied.

Fenton Hardy put a hand on Joe's shoulder. "Are you okay?" he asked.

Joe nodded.

"Did they get anything?" Harlan Dean asked.

"I don't know," Joe replied. "I guess Mr. Silvers will have to look around."

"We'll have to locate him," Mr. Tally said nervously. "And we'll report this to the police, immediately." He picked up the phone, then stopped and turned toward Fenton Hardy. "I certainly hope this won't cause you to consider choosing another hotel, Mr. Hardy. Our security is usually top—"

"We can discuss that later," Fenton said abruptly. "Right now I suggest you check to see if any other rooms have been . . . burgled."

"Of course." The assistant manager quickly signaled one of the security men to get on that, then he made his phone call.

Joe didn't miss the fact that his father had cut off the hotel worker deliberately. Why? he wondered. What was going on in the hotel, and how did it include Aunt Gertrude's friend?

Only one way to find out, Joe told himself. "What are you doing here, Dad?" he asked.

"Working." Fenton Hardy's answer was sharp and terse. "Why don't you head on home? I'll give your statement to the police. They can call if they need more information."

"Okay," Joe replied hesitantly. He wanted to stay to see what his father was hiding. But he also needed to tell Frank and Clayton Silvers what had happened.

"You can't describe your assailant?" Harlan Dean asked. Joe felt as if Dean was studying him. As if he knew Joe was keeping something back.

"No," Joe said. "I never got a look at him."

Dean nodded and turned back toward the window.

"You get on home and clean up," Fenton Hardy told his son. He gently placed a hand on Joe's shoulder. "Are you sure you're all right?" he asked sincerely.

"Sure I am, Dad."

"Okay, then," Fenton replied. "Please tell your aunt that I won't be home tonight. Business."

Joe looked over at Harlan Dean, then back at his father, but didn't say a word. He'd been here before. He knew his father had told him all he could or all he wanted to say.

When he left the hotel Joe found that his mind was racing. Had the man he fought with only been a burglar? It was possible. After all, the man had made sure to cover Joe's face when he attacked. The two men who had attacked Clayton had done so openly, Joe told himself. No masks. They hadn't even hidden their faces when they were staking out the Hardys' home.

Joe stepped out onto the sidewalk in front of the hotel and noticed the pieces of broken window glass on the ground. He glanced up at Clayton's window and saw his father watching him. Fenton waved, then turned away.

"This doesn't add up," Joe said softly. Did this have anything to do with the case their father was working on?

"So many new questions," Joe said as he hailed a cab. "And we haven't even found the answers to the first ones." He hoped Frank or Clayton and Aunt Gertrude were having better luck.

At that moment Frank Hardy was hoping the same thing about his younger brother. Frank had spent the last hour going through the newspaper morgue and questioning Darryl about Clayton Silvers's career.

Frank had even tried putting together a list of potential targets in the Bayport area. The list was a total of two: Orion Electronics and Fairmont Industries, two high-tech companies with labs just outside Bayport. Now he was hoping the tracking device they'd found would give them a major lead.

Frank pulled up in front of the familiar clapboard home of Phil Cohen, boy genius of Bayport. Phil had been a friend of the Hardys for years.

He was a nice guy, a wizard with electronics, and he'd helped the Hardys on many of their cases. Frank was hoping this would be another time when Phil would come through for them.

"Hey, Frank! What's up?" Phil greeted Frank with a cheerful, energetic slap on the back. "Have I got some amazing stuff to show you!"

"Whoa!" Frank said, holding his hands up. "Before you go there," he said, "something's come up, and we really need your help."

Frank showed Phil the small circular disk and told him everything that had happened over the past twenty-four hours.

"Whoa!" Phil exclaimed, after examining the device. "This is a major league tracking device. I mean, this is not your stereo store model."

"I know that," Frank said. "But I've never seen one quite like it. Where would you buy it?"

"No, no," Phil said enthusiastically as he led Frank down into his basement workshop. "You don't get it. This baby is two generations up from anything on the open market." Frank stared at Phil. "Frank, this is covert stuff, big bucks, spy guys!" Phil returned to examining the device under his magnifying glass. "Whoa," he repeated.

"What's the range of something like that?" Frank asked.

"With or without a Global Surveillance Satellite?"

Frank gave a soft whistle. "With."

"They could find us in Alaska or the Bahamas." Phil smiled. "And you know which one I'd rather be in."

"I don't think these thieves have access to a GSS," Frank said. "At least . . . I hope not."

Phil continued to examine the device like a child with a new toy. "Who are these guys?" he asked.

"That's what we have to figure out," Frank replied. "Can you find out anything about this unit? Where it came from? Who bought it? Where it's been? Anything?"

Now it was Phil's turn to throw up his hands. "Hold on there, Frank," he said. "I'm a whiz, true. But if these guys are as good as their technology, they'll have all kinds of shields. Phony names, cards, and stuff. It would be like tracking electronic ghosts."

Frank shrugged. "You're right, Phil," he said. "These guys are *really* good. There's no way that you could possibly get anything on them." He reached for the tracking device. "We'd need some *seriously* well-trained pro who could—"

"Wait a minute," Phil said, blocking Frank from

touching the device. "I didn't say I couldn't do it. I just said it would be hard."

Frank smiled. "Then go for it. Any information will help."

"Sure thing," Phil told him. "After all, my rep is on the line."

The two boys talked a little more as Phil walked Frank to the van.

"I've gotta tell you one thing," Phil said as Frank climbed in behind the wheel. "I hope these guys are just thieves and not anything else."

"Why?" Frank asked.

"Because with the kind of technology they have, they could listen in on anyone, track them anywhere, or destroy anything, and vanish without a trace."

9 Invasion

Joe Hardy pulled his brother into his room the moment Frank came home. He quickly told Frank about the attack at the hotel and how their father had reacted to the whole thing.

"Whoa!" Frank flopped down on Joe's bed and let out a low whistle. "What did Mr. Silvers say when you told him about this?"

"He was really quiet at first," Joe replied. "Especially when I mentioned Dad was there. Then he took off for the hotel. Said he'd check in with us later."

"And you think the guy you tackled could have something to do with Dad's case?" Frank asked.

"I don't know," Joe replied. "Dad's working on some kind of security job, and somehow it involves the hotel. Clayton Silvers is staying at the *same* hotel, and someone tried to search his room." Joe scratched his head. "I don't see how they connect, but it is possible."

Frank gazed out the window of Joe's room. The night sky was without stars and filled with thick, dark clouds. "Dad's client, Harlan Dean, acts like police or a federal agent," he said. "He could be looking for a fugitive, bodyguarding someone important, or transporting something valuable."

"Or dangerous," Joe added. He sat silently on his bed for a few seconds, then reached into his shirt pocket. "Then there's this thing," he said, pulling out the plastic card.

Frank took the card. "Where'd you get this?"

"The floor near the window," Joe explained. "At first I thought it was a credit card, but it's blank and has that one-by-two-inch strip of plastic hanging from it."

Frank noticed there were five individual wires running through the strip of plastic. They were evenly spaced, and like the strip they were torn at one end. "I think this is an electronic pass key," Frank said. "But I don't know what it was attached to."

"A passkey!" Joe's face lit up. "That could mean the assistant manager, Alfred Tally, could be involved. He would have access to passkeys for the hotel."

Frank's brow wrinkled as he recalled the first time he and Joe had met Alfred Tally. The man had been standoffish, Frank reminded himself, until he learned Joe and I were the sons of Fenton Hardy. "He did seem really interested in Mr. Silvers," Frank said to Joe. "In fact, he implied he'd been keeping tabs on the man for Dad."

"Maybe Dad and Harlan Dean are after Mr. Silvers," Joe offered. "After all, the authorities believe he's guilty. They might be trying to get more evidence on him."

"It's possible," Frank replied. "But between the attacks on Clayton, the tracking devices, and that car sabotage—I'm more worried about Aunt Gertrude. She's right in the middle."

"Maybe we should talk her into backing out of this," Joe suggested.

Frank smirked at his brother. "If you think we can, you need help."

"At least we have to try," Joe said. He stood up and headed for the bedroom door. "You coming?"

Frank shrugged. "Sure."

The boys found their aunt in the den, sitting at a dark oak wood desk. She was talking on the phone and had a large map of Bayport spread out in front of her. From the doorway, the boys could see that she had circled several areas on the map with a red marker. Most of them had been crossed out with an X. Only one had a check next to it, and Aunt

Gertrude, pen in hand, was poised over the last one.

"Are you sure, Millis?" she said, staring down at the map. "I need facts, not gossip." She paused for a moment. "All right then. Thank you. Yes, yes. I'll be there for the clothing drive next week. I'll be finished with my—project by then."

The boys waited patiently while their aunt exchanged a few more pleasantries, said goodbye, and hung up.

"You sound more sure of things than we do," Joe told her. "I didn't turn up anything on the thugs and their van."

"And I haven't learned much about that tracking device," Frank added. "Phil Cohen is working on it, though. He might call later, but we're not moving very fast."

"You two are so impatient," their aunt replied. She placed a check next to the last circled area on her map. "That's why I worry about you. You expect things to happen instantly."

"Well, that's the way a lot of our cases go," Joe said.

"Maybe so," Aunt Gertrude replied. "But not all the time. That is not how life works. Some things require patience, which I have. And because of that I've learned a few things in the past hour. Look at this."

Aunt Gertrude motioned for the boys to join her. They moved behind her so they could look over her shoulders. "Through the Rotary club and a friend who sells real estate, I found out that ten houses and motor homes have been rented in the past three weeks. Eight of them proved to be to families or college students. But the occupants of the last two rentals have been acting very odd. One is a writer, and the other works for that new TV cable company, Stellar Dish. In fact, I think he's the one who dropped by here the other day to check our service plan."

"How long was he here?" Frank asked.

"About twenty minutes, I'd say."

"Great!" Joe said enthusiastically. "We'll go check them out."

Aunt Gertrude whirled around to face him. "You will not!" she ordered. "Clayton and I will do that."

"But this could be dangerous," Frank pleaded. "We're better at—"

"You have no idea what experience is," Aunt Gertrude insisted. She took a deep breath, let it out, and then slowly removed her reading glasses. "I don't usually say this," she told the boys, "but I am very proud of you. You're compassionate and caring like your mother. You are clever and intelligent like your father." Gertrude Hardy glanced quickly at a framed photograph on the wall. It was an eight-by-ten picture of the last Hardy family reunion. Frank and Joe and their parents were in the photo, and so was Aunt Gertrude.

"Aunt Gertrude, we—"

Their aunt held up a hand for silence. "Back when we were teenagers, Clayton Silvers defended me." Frank and Joe exchanged glances.

"We worked together on a number of protest issues," Aunt Gertrude went on. "We fought for the environment, better education, and clean, affordable housing for the poor—we were friends, but there were differences, too. Places we did not go together. Friends and experiences we did not share."

"Because he was black and you were white?" Joe asked.

"We still are." Aunt Gertrude grinned. "But, yes, that was part of the problem. One day some people cornered me. They didn't like what Clayton and I were doing. They said we were spending too much time together. I felt certain that they were about to harm me, and I was as afraid as I had ever been."

"What happened?" Frank asked, sitting down on the edge of the desk and leaning in closer.

"Suddenly Clayton was there," Aunt Gertrude replied. "He stood with me. He didn't have to, but he did. Clayton told them whatever happened to me had to happen to him, and some of them would live to regret it. They closed in a step, and I felt certain a fight would break out. Then your father stepped in, too, and so did a few other people. The fight never happened. Thank goodness."

"Whew." Joe sighed. "That could have been ugly. But I bet you could have held your own."

"So that's why you're trying to clear Clayton Silvers," Frank said.

"No," Aunt Gertrude said with annoyance. "He was, is, and always will be my friend. *That's* why." Gertrude Hardy quickly rose from her chair.

"You boys are always ready to rush into danger," Aunt Gertrude said. "I told you that story so you would understand that I know something about danger and threats. I *know* what it is to lose someone you care about. I don't want to go through that again."

Frank and Joe were surprised by their aunt's statement. Her tale about Clayton did reveal another side of their friendship. But her remark about losing someone she cared about caught them off guard. What was she talking about? Whom had she lost?

Before Frank and Joe could ask the question, the doorbell rang.

Frank stayed with their aunt while Joe went to the front of the house and cautiously looked through the peephole. Instantly he threw open the door, and a wide-eyed Phil Cohen rushed into the house, carrying a backpack.

"Hey, Phil—"

Before Joe could finish speaking, Phil had clamped a damp hand over his mouth. Phil gestured for silence, just as Frank joined them. Catching their friend's signal, he watched as Phil pulled out a small electronic gadget from his backpack. It was the size of a hand-held computer game, but there were no colorful graphics or familiar characters. The view screen revealed an illuminated green grid with a series of circular bands pulsing around a tiny red dot. As Phil stepped farther into the hallway and turned toward the door to the den, two more red dots appeared, along with the same pulsating bands. Phil's face was tight with worry and possibly fear.

Frank and Joe watched as he pulled a folded sheet of paper from his coat pocket and handed it to them.

Huddled together, Frank and Joe read what was obviously a hastily written note from their friend. The impact of the last five words on the page struck the brothers with the force of a blow: "They know everything! Your house has been bugged!"

10 Nowhere Is Safe

The impact of Phil's note weighed heavily on the Hardys. They knew that if Phil was right, everything they had said, every plan, every suspicion had been overheard by the techno-thieves.

Joe suddenly realized they had been quiet far too long. He didn't want to tip off anyone listening, so he acted quickly. "Hey there, buddy," he said, patting Phil on the back a little harder than was necessary. "These mileage gauges will sure come in handy for the bike ride tomorrow."

Joe could see that Phil was confused, but Frank caught on instantly. "Yeah," he said nonchalantly. He grabbed a pen and some paper from a notepad by the door. "My gauge broke last month." He hastily scribbled a note to Phil telling him to play along. "Thanks for bringing this over."

The note read, "Go along with us on this while we search the place." Phil read the message and nodded. "No problem," he replied.

While Frank and Phil pretended to talk about schoolwork and friends, Joe pulled a chair under the smoke detector in the hallway. He carefully climbed up on the chair and examined the unit. A small microphone, no wider than a pencil and one-quarter the length, was hidden between the detector and the ceiling.

Frank found the second one that Phil's device indicated was there. It was hidden behind a ventilation grating, just inside the doorway to the dining room. They left both microphones in place.

"So, you want to hang out here for a while?" Joe asked Phil, still trying to decide what to do.

"If I'm going to hang out here," Phil said, pulling two more scanners from his backpack and giving them to the boys, "I need to know . . . if you guys have any snacks. I'm starved."

"Sure thing," Joe replied. He indicated that he would search the living room while Phil took the kitchen.

"I have to help Aunt Gertrude with something," Frank said. "But I'll only be in there a minute, so I'll meet you in the kitchen. Okay?"

The boys agreed, and each went off in his set direction.

When Frank entered the den, he signaled his aunt not to mention the device in his hand.

"Hey, Aunt Gertrude," Frank said as he handed her the note. "I was just thinking, you said one of the people on that map worked for the new cable company."

His aunt appeared nervous as she finished reading. "Uh, yes," she muttered.

"When did he stop by?" Frank began moving around, sweeping the room with Phil's scanner.

"Day before yesterday," Aunt Gertrude replied. Her voice was steadier.

"Well, no offense," Frank said. He turned and winked at her. "But Joe and I have been solving cases for a long time, and we just don't see how that guy could be involved."

"Oh, really?" Gertrude Hardy's brow wrinkled into a scowl.

"Yep." Frank had found another device hidden on top of a bookcase. "You'll get better at this if you stick with it."

Frank couldn't tell if the withering look his aunt gave him was because of the device he'd found or because of what he had said.

He hoped it was the first, not the latter.

After searching the house, the boys located six microphones. They also located a tracking device in the Hardys' van. They decided to leave them all connected—at least for now.

Finally Joe slipped into his room and turned on his CD player, and Frank turned on a radio in the kitchen, while Phil checked out the back porch. When he signaled that it was clear, the boys and Aunt Gertrude gathered out there.

"Why didn't you let me remove the bugs?" Phil asked Frank.

"Because that would alert the thieves that we were onto them. They might take off, and then we'd never catch them and clear Mr. Silvers."

"How did you know they'd bugged us?" Joe asked Phil.

"A hunch," Phil replied. "Once I realized the kind of equipment they had access to, it seemed logical."

"But when did they do it?" Aunt Gertrude asked. She looked a little stunned. Her eyes were wide with amazement.

"We've been out of the house a lot," Joe said. He turned to their aunt. "Have any strangers been by here in the past two days?"

"Not really," she replied. "There were Clayton, your father's client, Mr. Dean, a child selling magazine subscriptions, and the cable TV man."

"A cable guy?" Phil asked.

"Yes," Aunt Gertrude replied. "From the new company. They've taken over the accounts from the old cable company. They just wanted to check our service." Aunt Gertrude looked frightened. "Did I do the wrong thing?"

"No way," Joe told her. He put an arm around her shoulders.

"That makes the second time these guys have turned up in this case," Frank said. "It's time we checked them out."

"They came into our house," Aunt Gertrude said. She didn't really look at anyone. She stood there, numb, as if she couldn't believe her own words.

"Don't worry, Aunt Gertrude," Joe told her. "We found these bugs, and we'll figure out where the guys are hiding, too. We'll get 'em."

"Meanwhile," Frank added, "if you'd feel safer out of town, visiting a relative, I can call— "

Anger flashed in Gertrude Hardy's eyes. "No one is running me out of my own home!" she almost shouted, then caught herself. "No one."

Frank and Joe had never seen their aunt look so angry and determined.

"Then tomorrow we get serious," he said. "Joe and I will use our trail bike trip with Callie and Iola to check a couple of possible targets."

"Cool," Joe said. He turned to his aunt. "And you and Mr. Silvers can try to locate the point man's hideout."

"You bet we will," Aunt Gertrude said forcefully.

"Well, I'd better get back to my house and workshop," Phil said. "I want to see what else I can find out about that device."

Phil said good night to Aunt Gertrude, and she

strolled back into the kitchen. Frank and Joe walked Phil to his car and watched as he drove down the street. No car lights suddenly flicked on. There was no sudden screeching of tires as a pursuit car peeled away from the curb.

"Guess no one is following him," Frank said. "But the people we're up against could be watching from across town, and we wouldn't even know it. Spooky."

"We'll get 'em," Joe said. "We always do."

Aunt Gertrude suddenly came out the front door and joined the boys in the driveway. "It just occurred to me," she said cautiously. "If they could rap our home like that—"

"It's *tap*, Aunt Gertrude," Joe corrected her.

"That's not important, Joseph," she insisted. "If they can do that, couldn't they do the same to our phones? And if they have, how do I warn Clayton?"

"For now"—Frank rubbed his forehead in thought—"call him and say you have an idea you have to discuss with him tomorrow. Tell him it's important. Then Joe and I will go by the hotel in the morning to clue him in before your meeting."

Aunt Gertrude agreed and hurried back into the house.

"How are we going to keep in touch with everyone tomorrow if the home phone is bugged?" Joe asked.

"I have an idea about that," Frank said thoughtfully. He looked down the long dark street in both directions and felt a chill run through his body. "I sure wish Dad were going to be home tonight," he said.

Joe shrugged. "I told you, Dad said he was going to be working tonight and might not be home," he said. "Guess we're on our own."

Frank nodded. "Guess so."

The boys walked around the house a couple of times to make sure things were secure, then they went inside. An hour later, as they all turned in for the night, they locked doors and windows but didn't feel the least bit secure.

Frank and Joe rose early the next morning and found Aunt Gertrude had already prepared a breakfast of blueberry pancakes, ham, and orange juice.

"You'll be cycling all over creation today, and you'll need a good meal for energy," she told the brothers.

Though she was doing a good job of acting normally, Joe could see the effect of the strain on his aunt. These guys better hope the police get to them before I do, he told himself.

He and Frank played their parts well. They pretended that the trail bike ride was the only plan they had for the day. "We can work on Mr. Silvers's case after our ride," Joe told Frank.

The boys ate quickly, then watched as Aunt Gertrude left in her loaner car to go visit a friend. They didn't want her home by herself. After a few minutes they followed her on their bikes, keeping a sharp eye out for the white van or Land Rover, signs of danger.

Once they were sure she was safe, the boys headed into downtown Bayport.

"You think our home security system will keep those guys out?" Joe asked Frank.

"They really have no reason to go in there now," he replied. "But it should work. After all, security is one of Dad's specialties."

They pulled up in front of the Bayport Plaza Hotel and chained their bikes to a lamppost. Walking into the lobby, the Hardys felt a strange tension in the air. Everything looked normal. The bellhops were helping guests with their luggage. The concierge was suggesting places of interest to a tourist couple. Several businessmen were chatting or reading papers.

As he and Frank stood waiting for the elevator, Joe glanced at one of the men reading a paper. The headline declared, "Defense Committee Session Starts Today." He vaguely remembered that one of their local politicians was somehow involved in those sessions just before the elevator doors opened up.

"You get a creepy feeling in the lobby?" Joe asked as they took the elevator to the fifth floor.

Frank nodded. "I thought it was just me. Weird."

The elevator doors opened, and Joe and Frank stepped out on the fifth floor. The corridor was carpeted, with small electric sconces hanging at intervals along the walls. It was very quiet.

"What's his new room number?" Frank asked.

"He told Aunt Gertrude it's right across from his old room," Joe replied. "Hotel said they'd fix the window in the old one and he could move back in if he wanted to."

When they reached Clayton Silvers's room, they pulled out the scanner Phil had lent them and a note they had written to Clayton. It opened with the line "Your room has been bugged" in big bold letters. Then it explained the events of the previous night.

Joe knocked, and Silvers opened the door quickly. "Hey there, you two," he said cheerfully. "Come on in. I was just about to shave."

Clayton wore a pair of beige slacks and a powder blue shirt, open at the neck. There was a bath towel draped around his shoulders, and he held an electric shaver in one hand. He noticed the devices in the boys' hands, but before he could speak, Joe showed him the note.

"We can't stay," Frank said, easing past the reporter while he read the note. Joe followed Frank in, and they began searching the room. "Aunt Gertrude just wanted us to give you a list of places she thought you should check out before you meet this afternoon," he said.

In seconds the boys had found one microphone behind a picture hanging on the wall and another in the light fixture, just above the bathroom medicine cabinet.

"Well, thanks for that," he said. His voice did not reveal the anger the boys could see on his face. "I have to shave and go keep an appointment. But I'll be back in time to meet your aunt."

"Good," Joe said, heading for the door. "We'll call you later."

Clayton signaled the boys to wait outside in the hallway. He then closed the door, and the Hardys could tell he'd switched on his electric shaver. The high-pitched buzz filtered through the metal door. A moment later Clayton eased the door open, slipped out to join them, but did not let the door close completely.

"How's your aunt taking all of this?" he asked.

"She's pretty mad," Joe replied. "But she wants these guys caught and your name cleared."

Clayton smiled. "That's Spitfire, all right," he said. "I'm sorry I've brought all of this down on your family. I never meant to."

"Don't worry about it, sir," Frank said. He seemed uneasy as he asked, "We were wondering, though . . . are the police still trying to prove you guilty?"

Clayton sighed and leaned against the wall. "Not really," he said. "I'm not worth the authorities' time."

"Did our dad keep an eye on you last night?" Frank asked.

"He had hotel security check on me," Clayton replied. "But I haven't seen him since he left here yesterday. I had the feeling things were kind of busy here last night. Didn't see much, but I just had that feeling."

"We got that same feeling when we came in just now," Joe said. "Well, thanks anyway."

Clayton still held the Hardys' note in his hand. He glanced at it, then back at his room. "I agree we should leave them in place for now, but this is going to cramp our movements."

"Not necessarily," Frank said. "We gave Aunt Gertrude one of our cell phones. When you two go check out those suspects, we can keep in touch that way."

"Your aunt worries about you two—a lot," Clayton told them. "I think she's afraid of losing someone close again."

"Wait a minute," Joe said. "The other day Aunt Gertrude said she didn't want to lose someone else. What was she talking about?"

Clayton Silvers looked down at the floor, then glanced at the door to his room. "I don't know that it's my place to tell you that," he said, facing the boys.

"We love our aunt," Frank told the reporter. "We don't want to hurt her or make her worry. Maybe if we understood this, we could make things easier for her."

Clayton still hesitated.

"We're not children, Mr. Silvers," Joe said, quietly. "Not anymore."

Clayton sighed heavily. "Your aunt was engaged once, to a really great guy."

The boys looked stunned but said nothing.

"He was a businessman with a small store that was doing okay," Clayton continued. "But it needed help. Your aunt went to work for him, which is how they met. Her savvy helped the business grow. In fact, it made a nice bit of change." Clayton shifted uneasily from one foot to the other. "Two months before the wedding, he went on a business trip—and the plane crashed."

"He didn't make it?" Joe asked.

Clayton nodded his head. "Your aunt was hurting for a long time after that. It was even harder when she found out he'd left the business to her in his will."

"What happened to it?" Frank asked.

"Your aunt didn't want to be there anymore," Clayton replied. "Too many memories. So, she sold it." Clayton Silvers shoved his hands into his pockets with obvious irritation. "I wasn't much help," he said. "I was there at first, but I soon took off. I had this big career to get back to. Headlines to grab! That's why I didn't know where you were. Some friend."

"Doesn't look like she's holding anything against you, too much," Frank said.

Clayton grinned. "That's not her style. Not Spitfire."

"We'd better go," Joe said, glancing at his watch. "We still have to pick up Callie and Iola."

"Okay," Clayton said. "I'll let you know what I find out later."

"Be careful," Frank told him.

Clayton chuckled. "Funny—that's what I was going to tell you."

Clayton Silvers slipped back into his room and quietly closed the door as the Hardys took the elevator down to the first floor.

Walking across the lobby, the boys sensed a kind of tension once again.

Joe glanced around the room. It looked the same. A couple of the tourists were still there, glancing through brochures. The businessmen were still scattered about the room, talking or reading their newspapers. Ordinary-looking people, Joe thought. One of the tourists and two of the businessmen wore glasses and hearing aids. Same activities and same— Then it hit him, but he didn't say anything until they were out on the street.

"Did you spot it, Frank?" he asked his brother.

"Spot what?"

"The setup." Joe waited for the light to go on in Frank's eyes. "The same guests in pretty much the same places—with hearing aids."

Frank snapped his fingers. "Security!" he exclaimed through clenched teeth. "Most of those guys were plainclothes security men, planted around the lobby. That's why we felt the tension."

"Which means that whatever Dad is working on came in last night, and is probably still in the hotel."

"Darryl said someone important was coming into the airport last night," Frank said as they unchained their bikes. "He and some reporter were rushing out to try for an interview."

"Do you suppose Dad's case ties in with Clayton's?"

"I don't see how," Frank replied. "But then again, anything is possible. Let's think about it while we ride over to Callie's. Maybe we'll have some answers by the time we get there."

But when the boys reached Callie Shaw's home, there were only more questions waiting for them. More questions, and a great deal of fear.

"We're glad you're here, Frank," Callie said as she led the Hardys into her room. Iola Morton was sitting on the floor, staring up at the computer on the white lacquered desk. She jumped up when Joe came in.

"Do you believe this?" Iola said, her voice shrill.

"What's wrong?" Joe and Frank asked in unison.

Callie pointed to the computer screen. "Look," she said.

The image on the screen was the same blue and orange graphics Frank had seen hundreds of times when he signed on to get E-mail from his server. He and Callie and many of their school friends used the same server. It came with a lot of neat extras that made it fun to use.

But this image was not fun. An E-mail had been opened, and its message had been written in bold, colorful letters.

"Tell the boys to back off," it read. "Or they can kiss the girls . . . goodbye."

11 "SEARCH"

"Kiss us goodbye!" Iola Morton shouted. Her slender hands were clenched into tight fists trembling at her sides. "What do they think we are—disposable or something?"

"Calm down," Joe Hardy suggested, then realized his mistake. Iola had quite a temper, and he had just said the one thing she hated most.

"Calm down!" she exclaimed. "I'll calm down when I've tied their arms and legs in knots!"

"Iola got one of these at her house just before she came over here," Callie explained. There was tension in her voice, and Frank knew she was as upset as Iola.

"How'd they get our E-mail addresses?" Iola asked.

"I'm not sure," Frank replied. He sat down at Callie's computer and scrolled to the bottom of the E-mail. The electronic footnotes on the bottom suggested the E-mail originated from an education source. "I doubt these guys are local college students pulling a prank," Frank said. "So they probably routed this message through a local university server via satellite."

"So you think they somehow accessed our hard drive and copied our E-mail address book," Joe suggested. "Then they routed their message through a shadow system, so we couldn't trace it. These guys are good!"

Frank turned away from the screen. "I'll check on that when we get back to the house later," he said. "The question now is, what do we do about this threat?"

"Don't you *dare* think about backing off, Frank," Callie said firmly. "Not because of us."

"But—"

"I mean it, Frank."

"Callie's right!" Iola insisted. "You catch these guys so I can give them more than a piece of my mind."

Joe gently squeezed Iola's hand. "We'll get them, and you can have what's left."

"Okay then." Frank rose from the chair. "If we're going to nail these guys, let's get started. We've got a lot of ground to cover."

"Where to?" Callie asked as she grabbed her backpack.

"A leisurely ride through the countryside . . . to ask some questions at Orion Electronics or Fairmont Industries. They are the two most likely places around for techno-thieves to rob," Frank said.

"Well, let's get going, Frank!" Joe grabbed Iola's backpack and rushed for the door. There was a twinkle in his eye. "We've got some miles to cover—and it's going to be hard for the girls to keep up."

"Oh, really?" Iola snatched her bike helmet up from the floor and raced after him. "I'll show you, Joe Hardy!"

Frank noticed Callie staring up at him. "I didn't say a word," he said sheepishly.

"A good thing, too." Callie smiled. "Let's go."

Callie picked up her backpack, jacket, and helmet, and with Frank joined the others outside. A few minutes later the four teens were riding north into the mountains that rose behind the town.

With Joe and Iola in the lead, they took a narrow rutted road that headed east into a dense wooded area.

The Hardys had picked this trail for two reasons. It was one of the more picturesque routes through the area. Everywhere they looked, tall cedar, pine, and maple trees reached toward the sky, and the wild-life was plentiful. And though it was the long way around, the trail would eventually bring them to the road that ran right past Orion Electronics. There was a junior executive there whom they had once helped out of a jam. They were sure she would talk to them.

The other reason was more practical. It would be impossible for anyone to follow them in a van or truck over the rough terrain. If they used motor-bikes, the sound would travel over great distances.

Most of the ride was fun and exciting. Callie and Iola were great at trail biking. They sometimes raced the boys on a straight strip of road. Other times, they stopped to watch deer in the distance.

The morning was filled with laughter and discovery. Only now and then did Joe or Frank check back down the trail to make sure they were not being followed.

As he rode, Frank wondered how they could stop the thieves. He and Joe had no idea where they would strike, or how. And so far, the thieves had proved to be intelligent, well-equipped, and dangerous. They had the advantage of knowing all the players in the game, while he and Joe had only seen two of the men. He suspected there had to be at least one more.

Joe replayed the attack at the hotel. Had he missed some important clue? Who dropped the broken master key? One of the thieves or Mr. Tally, the assistant manager? Was Tally part of the plot? He *had* been watching Clayton Silvers. Joe also wondered how his father fit into this mystery. Did he suspect Clayton was really guilty? Or was there more to it?

Both brothers worried about the threat to Callie and Iola, though the girls never mentioned it once on the ride. With Aunt Gertrude working with Clayton, too many people they cared about were in the line of fire.

By the time the teens reached the main road, the boys were convinced that no one would be safe until they had nailed these crooks. And they knew that that had to be soon—or it would be too late.

Fifteen minutes on the well-paved road, and the group could see Orion Electronics in the distance. The four-story steel-and-glass structure was about a block long. The tinted glass reflected the bright noonday sun like a wall of mirrors.

"Half the animals in this area must be blind by now," Joe said. Even with his sunglasses on, he had to squint to see the building.

"They're probably smart enough not to stare at the building," Iola teased. "Unlike some people I could name."

She nudged Joe playfully, then sped off on her bike. "I'll beat you there!"

"I don't think so!" Joe shouted. He was off in a flash with Frank and Callie right on his tail.

The guard at the front gate was not amused when the four teens skidded to a stop near his small booth. Their wheels kicked up a shower of gravel and dirt.

"Sorry about that," Frank told the man.

The guard was a little standoffish until Frank explained whom they had come to see. After a phone call to the executive the teens were allowed to leave their bikes with the guard and go inside the complex. Ms. Waylan was pressed for time, but she spoke freely to the Hardys after they voiced their concerns. Still, by the time they left the complex, they had no more to go on than when they had arrived.

"That was a bust," Joe complained as they retrieved their bikes. "They're not working on anything hush-hush that might interest our techno-thieves."

"Are you sure she was telling you the truth?" Callie asked.

"I think so," Frank replied. "She had no reason to lie. She could have just said she couldn't talk about it and that they'd take the proper precautions." He seemed troubled by something. "Still . . . I don't know."

"They haven't hired any new employees either," Iola added. "So what do we do now?"

Frank straddled his bike and began to pedal back to the road. "We go over to Fairmont Industries to see what they have to say," he said, then grew quiet.

"What's up, big brother?" Joe asked as he rode beside him.

"I feel like we have all the pieces to this puzzle," Frank replied. "But I don't have any idea how to put them together."

"Want to go over everything?" Joe asked.

"Not yet," Frank said. "Let's wait until after we leave Fairmont."

Joe agreed, and for the next half-hour they rode southeast toward their next destination. Once again, they kept to the rougher trails and checked to make certain they were not being followed.

Around two o'clock they stopped in a meadow to have lunch. A gentle breeze rustled the leaves and branches. Though Frank and Joe wanted to sit and enjoy the afternoon, they ate quickly, and by three o'clock they were riding onto the manicured grounds of Fairmont Industries. The grass was evenly cut, the bushes trimmed and shaped. Even the branches of the thin birch trees seemed to have been trimmed to the same basic size and form.

Fairmont appeared to be as successful as Orion Electronics. A large black-and-gold metal sign stood on the lawn by the entrance. The main buildings were mostly white stone with few windows.

"Looks like the employees don't get a lot of sun around here," Joe commented.

"They work on special computer chips and other light-sensitive technology," Frank explained as they chained their bikes to an employee bike rack. "Too much sun, too few profits."

Joe shrugged and followed Frank, Callie, and Iola into the building.

After showing ID and speaking with security, the

boys and their friends were shown up to the office of the executive they'd come to see, Mark Lowry.

Once again the interview was polite, sincere, but brief.

"Sorry I can't be of any help," Mr. Lowry said as he walked them to the front door. "No new projects or employees. And the head of our security has been with us over five years."

"Well, thanks for your time and the tour," Joe told the executive.

"You boys and your father saved us a bundle last year," Mr. Lowry said as they stepped outside. "We owe you. Come by anytime."

The Hardys said their goodbyes and were about to leave when Frank remembered the electronic master key in his backpack.

"Maybe you can help us with this," he said, handing the card to the executive. "Can you tell me anything about it?"

Mr. Lowry studied the blank card, then the attached strip of plastic and wires. "This is a master passkey," he said slowly. "Though I'm surprised to see it in this condition."

"Why?" Joe asked.

"Because this is part of a very expensive unit," Mr. Lowry replied. He held up the torn strip. "This piece attaches to a box-shaped unit about the size of a paperback book. You insert the card into any electronic card lock, and the box decodes the combination."

"Any combination?" Joe asked. "Like the doors in a hotel?"

Mr. Lowry nodded. "Though I'd be surprised to see it used that way."

"Really?" Iola said.

"This is top of the line," he said. "Only top security and intelligence professionals would have one of these. Not anyone in basic hotel security, unless they were *very* well connected."

Frank and Joe exchanged glances.

"Thanks, Mr. Lowry," Frank told the executive. "I think you've just given us our first real lead."

Mr. Lowry still had a puzzled expression on his face as the four teens rode away from the complex.

"Do you think that the hotel assistant manager, Mr. Tally, is in with the thieves?" Joe asked his brother.

"I think that's a good thing to find out today," Frank replied. He led the group back to Bayport. The late afternoon air had turned chilly and cut through their windbreakers.

The teens exchanged ideas and questions about the case, all the way back to town. By the time the Hardys dropped Callie and Iola off at their homes, they felt sure the criminals would strike soon.

"So now we go check out that cable TV company," Joe said. "Right?"

Frank frowned. "Guess so," he replied. "They must tie into this somewhere."

"But if they're not after either of the two electronic companies," Joe said in frustration, "what is worth their time in Bayport?"

"Mr. Silvers said it was something really big," Frank replied. "And they're moving fast to get us out of the way."

"Yeah," Joe agreed. "They tried to kidnap Mr. Silvers and bump him off even with our aunt in the car. Then they bug our house, all in twenty-four hours."

Joe's statement caused Frank to pause. "All in twenty-four hours . . ." he mused. "I don't think that's possible. I mean, how could—"

Frank's question was cut off by the ringing of Joe's cell phone.

"Joe here," he said into the cellular unit.

"Yo, Joe, my man," a voice announced cheerfully. "Darryl here."

Joe signaled Frank, and they both pulled over to the curb. "What's up, Darryl?"

"Frank asked me to let him know if I found out anything about the places those techno-thieves hit or the frame job on Mr. Silvers. Right?"

"Right."

"So, I did," Darryl replied. "Seems the very place that Mr. Silvers thought they'd hit, they did . . . exactly one week after Mr. Silvers was fired."

"How'd they do it?"

"Nobody knows," Darryl replied. "They snatched some mega-important materials right out of the company's code-encrypted computer files without setting off any alarms. Even their security consultant couldn't figure it out."

"Can you find out who their security consultant was?" Joe asked. "Maybe he can tell us something."

"I'll try," Darryl replied anxiously. "But not right now. I'm running out with one of the reporters on a story. Some political bigwig is in town, but it's being kept very hush-hush."

"Who?" Joe asked.

"We think it's Congressman Reynolds," Darryl replied. "We missed him at the airport, but we'll find out sooner or later."

"Well, thanks for the help." Joe said.

"No problem," Darryl replied. "What are you guys going to do?"

"Check out that new cable company on Beale Street," Joe replied. "We think they may be involved."

"Okay," Darryl said. "But remember, I get a crack at the story. It's a good way for me to make points around here."

Joe agreed, then said goodbye. He checked in with his aunt and told her where they were going, then turned to Frank. "Where does this news about the robbery fit in?" he asked his brother.

"I'm not sure," he said as they started pedaling down the street. "But I'm sure it does."

"We need to start separating the false clues from

the true ones," Joe said. "Let's get over to Stellar Dish TV and see what they can tell us."

The Stellar Dish TV Cable Company was located in a one-story redbrick building in the old section of Bayport's business district. The entrance was off the parking lot in front, next to a large picture window. Frank and Joe noticed a truck bay in back of the shop, but there were no white vans in sight. In fact, the parking lot was as deserted as the street, and they didn't see anyone through the window.

"I know it's after five, but it sure is quiet," Joe said.

Frank nodded.

The boys pushed open the dark green metal door and walked inside. The room was small. There was a counter directly in front of them and another door behind it. A few empty chairs sat to their right, next to a vending machine. But there appeared to be no one in the room. Frank called out, but no one answered.

"This is where the hero usually says something's wrong," Joe teased with an element of tension in his voice.

Again Frank nodded. He motioned for Joe to follow him as he went behind the counter to push open the door a crack.

Peeking through the opening, the boys could see part of a large work and storage area. The muscles in Frank's stomach tightened. They should back off, he thought. This felt too much like a trap. But if the

110

crooks were here, and not expecting them, then it was a great chance to get some real evidence.

Exchanging a cautious glance with Joe, Frank stepped into the room. Joe was only a few feet behind him.

Two walls of the room were lined with boxes and shelves. More boxes were stacked on the floor. One wall held a series of workstations with benches and tools for working on electronic equipment. The fourth wall was two corrugated steel garage doors. The boys assumed that outside these doors was where the vans loaded.

Joe stepped up to Frank. "Smell that?" he asked.

Frank detected a strong, familiar odor. But before he could reply, the lights went out.

The blow was swift, hard, and efficient. Joe felt his legs go weak, and the room began to whirl. Frank felt nothing as he fell to the floor.

Joe wanted to lift his head from the floor but couldn't. He couldn't move any part of his body, and nothing in the dark room seemed real. Except the odor. Familiar, nauseating. He realized what it was just as the room lit up in bright yellow and red lights. No, not lights—flames. The room had been set on fire.

"Frank," Joe moaned. Then, as the fire burned brighter, everything went black.

12 Escape

His face was on fire.

That was the first thought that flashed through Joe Hardy's mind as consciousness returned. The right side of his face was hot, as if he were lying next to an oven.

But worse than the heat was the smoke. Joe was choking. His legs and body felt sluggish, and he could barely move. Yet something was tugging at him—pulling, in fact.

"Come on, Joseph, please!" The frantic voice shouting in his ear belonged to Aunt Gertrude. Joe's eyes began to focus, and he saw the terror-filled expression on her face. "Please, Joseph!"

Aunt Gertrude pulled desperately on his shirtfront

until she had him in a sitting position. "We have to go," she pleaded. "The room is on fire!"

Clarity blazed before Joe as he painfully scrambled to his feet. There were flames everywhere. Tools and equipment, boxes of wire, cable, and brochures all burned brightly—releasing poisonous fumes.

Joe leaned on his aunt's shoulder as they stumbled toward the door. For a split second Joe thought he saw something, but a coughing fit took hold of him as his aunt rushed them from the room.

"Where's Frank?" Joe gasped.

"Clayton has him," Aunt Gertrude replied. She was also choking, and Joe could hear the terror in her voice. "Hurry!"

Gertrude Hardy led them through the outer room and into the parking lot and fresh air.

The cool night air and the sight of Frank a few feet ahead of him revived Joe further. Frank was leaning against a dark blue sedan, and Clayton Silvers was with him. The moment he saw them, the reporter rushed to help Aunt Gertrude and Joe.

"You okay, Frank?" Joe gasped.

"Except for a headache and some singed hair, I'm fine." Frank tried to grin but winced from some pain he felt. He reached up and touched the back of his head.

"Did one of the cable workers do this?" Clayton asked. "Are they involved?"

"I didn't see who hit me," Joe replied. Frank

agreed. "We walked in and—" Suddenly Joe scrambled to his feet and half ran, half stumbled back to the burning building.

"Joe!" Aunt Gertrude screamed.

"One of the workers," Joe called back. "I saw one of them in there!"

Joe raced through the outer room and into the back area. Dizziness almost overcame him and caused him to fall into a stack of blazing boxes. The smoke was thick, dense, causing his eyes to burn and his lungs to scream for air. He couldn't see the worker.

"Where was he?"

Joe whirled around and saw Frank stumbling in behind him.

"Over that way," Joe said, coughing periodically.

Holding their jackets up to shield their faces from the flames, the Hardys rushed over to an area near the workbenches. There on the floor, half under one of the workbenches, they spotted a crumpled form.

Joe and Frank grabbed the body and dragged it from the room as fast as they could. Once outside, Clayton helped lay the man down by his rental car, while Aunt Gertrude talked to the police on her cell phone.

While Clayton administered first aid, the Hardys stared at the burning building.

"It burned too fast to be anything but deliberate," Frank said.

"That's for sure," Joe replied. "Remember the smell—gasoline?"

Frank nodded. In the distance he could hear the sounds of police sirens. "We were lucky," Frank muttered.

"Yeah, we were," Joe replied. A squad car and fire trucks came screaming down the street and pulled in next to the building.

Soon the EMS unit arrived, and after a few minutes the medics revived the man Frank and Joe had pulled from the flames. The boys quickly learned his name was John Andrews, and he was the owner of the company.

Mr. Andrews sat up on the gurney inside the ambulance, with a small oxygen mask over his face.

"They tell me you saved my life," Andrews mumbled through the mask. "I don't know how to thank you."

"That's okay," Frank said. "Someone saved us, too."

"Can you tell us what happened to you?" Joe asked.

The man shrugged and appeared to be confused and worried. "It was weird," he said. "Some guy comes in saying he wants to order our service. While I'm handing him the order forms, I hear a noise from behind me, in the back room. I turn around to look, and bang! I'm hit from behind."

"The customer hit you," Frank said.

"Only person it could have been," the man replied.

"I only have two other guys working for me, and they were out."

"Can you remember anything about that man?" Frank asked.

The man shook his head slowly. "Not really. He was slim, had brown hair, and was a slob. Nothing special."

"A slob?" Frank asked.

"He'd smeared some reddish stuff on his shirt. Looked like jelly or something. Even had some on his hands. Made the order forms sticky."

Just then the EMS technician came to the back of the ambulance. "We want to take you all to the hospital for examination, so—"

"We're fine," Joe protested as he and Frank hopped down out of the vehicle.

"You should get checked out—"

"And they will," Aunt Gertrude declared as she walked up to the group. "I want to know you and Frank are completely healthy."

"We promise we'll go, but just not now," Frank insisted. "We believe that whatever is going to happen will go down tonight. We've got to stay on this— or none of us will be safe, and Mr. Silvers's career will be over."

Reluctantly, Aunt Gertrude agreed, and the EMS worker climbed into the ambulance with Mr. Andrews. The vehicle pulled away, siren lights flashing.

"Where's Mr. Silvers?" Frank asked his aunt.

"He's using the cell phone to gather more information," she said. "Why do you think the thieves will strike tonight?"

"They've tried kidnapping, sabotage, eavesdropping, and now murder," Frank explained. "They must think we're getting close."

"And whatever they're after is a big score," Joe added.

"Well, what do we know so far?" Aunt Gertrude asked.

"We know their target isn't a bank, electronics corporation, government laboratory, or Internet theft," Clayton Silvers said as he joined the group. He snapped the cell phone shut. "My snitch just told me his street and Web sources are pretty sure of that. He has one more source to check, then we'll meet."

Aunt Gertrude looked irritated. "We also know that the two suspects we thought we found turned out to be completely innocent."

"I'm sure we're up against at least three men," Joe said. "The man who attacked me at the hotel was thinner than the two thugs who tried to kidnap Mr. Silvers."

"One of those two likes doughnuts," Frank added. "We saw a box of them on the dashboard when they were watching our house, and later when they sabotaged Aunt Gertrude's car."

"Then there's the stuff we found out today," Joe said.

He and Frank told Clayton Silvers and their aunt everything that had happened—including the E-mail threats and the electronic master key.

"Something's been bothering me," Clayton Silvers said. He'd been watching the firefighters water down the smoldering embers and poke among the charred walls. He turned to Frank and Joe. "How come these guys have been concentrating on you two?"

The Hardy boys looked puzzled.

"Because we're working on the case," Joe replied.

"So am I," Clayton said. "For over a year. Why haven't they come after me more than they have? It's as if they think you pose a greater threat."

Frank's eyes grew wide. "Because of our father!" he exclaimed. "Joe and I had a feeling his case and ours were connected."

"So do I," Clayton agreed. "Is he protecting that guy Dean? I've seen him somewhere before."

"He's from Washington," Aunt Gertrude remarked. "Maybe you saw him there."

"I'll call a friend of mine and ask some questions," Clayton offered as he began dialing a number on the cell phone.

Suddenly Frank grabbed the phone. "How stupid!"

"Excuse me?" Clayton said.

"Phil kept saying these guys are pros, with high-tech surveillance equipment! Why didn't I get it?"

"They can monitor our cell phone calls!" Joe shouted.

"Is that possible?" Aunt Gertrude asked. "I mean there are no wires."

"And each call is encoded so people can't just listen in," Clayton observed.

"With the right technology, a satellite hookup, and decoder," Frank explained, "they can pull a signal right out of the air."

"Oh no!" Clayton exclaimed. He suddenly ran around his car and jumped into the driver's seat. "I was talking to my snitch on your phone! We arranged to meet on a street corner near here."

Joe jumped in beside Clayton, and Frank slipped into the backseat.

"And if those guys overheard that call—" Joe said.

Clayton violently twisted the ignition key "He's a dead man."

13 Program for Destruction

"His name is Willie T," Clayton Silvers explained as he sped through the streets of Bayport. Joe sat to his right, and Frank was in the backseat. Aunt Gertrude had stayed back at the scene of the fire to alert the police and Fenton Hardy.

"A reporter friend of mine told me about him when I said I was coming to Bayport," Clayton continued.

"He's a stoolie, here in our town?" Joe asked.

"Willie prefers to be called an information facilitator." Clayton exaggerated the last two words. "He'll be called DOA if we don't get there in time."

The car sped down narrow streets with old four-story buildings. This was a popular area for college students and artists. The rents were low, and the old postwar buildings had what some called character. Only every third street lamp worked, and few of the scrawny trees were healthy with leaves.

Beyond the six-block region stood a large above-ground parking lot and the warehouse district. There were a few stores and fast food restaurants scattered about. Just up the street, Willie T came around the corner and stopped in front of a café.

"That's him," Clayton called out. He pressed down on the accelerator as something else happened. Across the street, just beyond Willie, a set of head-lights came on as a parked Land Rover leaped away from the curb.

"They're going for him!" Joe exclaimed. He saw the vehicle racing toward Willie.

Without a word, Clayton jammed his foot down on the gas pedal and aimed his car at the would-be killers. At the last possible second, Clayton slammed on the brakes. "Hold on!"

Joe leaped into the backseat as the car screeched to a stop between Willie and the oncoming vehicle.

The driver of the Land Rover swerved to avoid crashing. His bumper scraped along the side of Clayton's car, tearing up paint and steel.

Frank caught a glimpse of the two men in the car as it sped away. It was the same two thugs with their doughnut box and all.

Clayton leaped from the car. "Willie, are you all right?"

The short, thin informant slowly rose to his feet, his hands and knees trembling. "You know I get extra for near-death experiences," he said, a slight smile on his face.

"Stay with him," Frank called out as he leaped into the driver's seat. "We'll try to follow those guys!"

With Joe in the back and his tires screeching, Frank executed a U-turn and took off in pursuit of the bad guys.

But before the boys reached the first corner, the crooks had executed two other turns and were out of sight. The Hardys had no idea which way to go. They drove around for a few minutes, then gave up.

Frank slammed his fist on the dashboard. "These guys are really starting to get to me," he said.

"And we have no idea where to go next," Joe added.

Frank took a deep breath and let it out slowly. "Maybe we do," he said. "But first . . ." He turned the car around and went back to see if Willie and Clayton were still on the corner.

"Good, they're gone," Frank told Joe. "Remember I said we had all the pieces but didn't know how to put them together?"

Joe nodded.

"Try this." Frank pulled away from the curb and drove back toward Bayport's downtown area. "The thieves' point man came here to scout out the area for their big job," Frank mused. "They figure Dad might be a problem because—"

"He's already been called in on the case," Joe chimed in.

"Right," Frank said. The car sped up. "They need to know what he's up to, so they bug the house before we even met Clayton Silvers."

"Sure," Joe said. "Aunt Gertrude said the cable guy was there a couple of days ago, but only for about twenty minutes. Not enough time to bug the whole house like that."

"So Dad's client is the target," Frank says. "But who is his client? And who is the third man in the gang?"

"That guy at Fairmont Industries said that hotel security wouldn't have an electronic master key like the thing I found," Joe said thoughtfully. "But if Tally is part of the gang, he'd have access to one. And he'd be in a perfect place to go after Dad's client since it has something to do with the hotel."

"That's why we're going there . . ." Frank turned into the parking lot of the Bayport Plaza Hotel. "Right now."

It took the boys a few minutes before they located Mr. Tally in one of the meeting rooms.

The assistant manager grew nervous and tense when he saw the boys enter. "Please don't tell me you've encountered another prowler," he pleaded.

Frank stared at the man. "Worse, Mr. Tally," he said. "We know that the prowler wasn't after cash or jewelry. He was working with the people we . . . uh, our dad is after."

"And he left an important clue behind," Joe added. "We found it, and now we know who we're—"

"Then you'll arrest Mr. Silvers immediately?" Mr. Tally's eyes grew wide. "You'll get him before he tries to blackmail the congressman."

"Excuse me?" Joe said.

"Well, we certainly don't want him to do to Congressman Reynolds what he did to those other people in Washington," Mr. Tally insisted. "Not in our hotel."

"You were watching Mr. Silvers to protect Congressman Reynolds?" Frank asked. "He's here in Bayport?"

Mr. Tally stared at Frank for a moment. "Of course he is. Isn't that why I was asked to keep watch on Mr. Silvers?"

"Is the congressman in the building now?" Frank asked urgently.

"Well, no. He's gone to his meeting." Tally appeared annoyed. "I'm sure I don't know why they couldn't hold their meeting here at the hotel, instead of some secret—"

"Oh, no," Joe said through clenched teeth. "Come on, Frank."

But Frank was moving almost before his brother spoke. They both knew that their father would never have asked Mr. Tally to watch Clayton Silvers. If he suspected Clayton of something, he would have watched the man himself. The boys also knew that

Congressman Reynolds was in the public eye right now for a very serious reason. He was heading up a committee looking into the efficiency of the National Defense System. That committee would be reviewing all early warning systems and defense plans . . . all of them.

Frank and Joe ran from the hotel and leaped into the car. As Joe gunned the engine, he knew he shared his brother's thoughts and fears. If they didn't move fast and get it all right, the security of the United States was about to go up in a cloud—of nuclear smoke.

14 Ground Zero

"We'll never find where Dad is holding this meeting." Joe spoke rapidly as he steered Silvers's car through the evening twilight. "So we've got to find these techno-thieves before they strike. But how?"

"No time. Should we go back for Silvers? Head back to the warehouse district," Frank told his brother. "I have an idea." Frank slammed his fist into the palm of his other hand. "How come we didn't see this before?"

"Because it was tricky," Joe replied. "Now it looks like Congressman Reynolds came here to speak with someone. Probably about his defense committee work."

"Most likely Senator Ogilvy," Frank suggested.

"He's not only on the committee, he's kind of a hold-out. He doesn't want our rights to personal privacy violated in the name of national defense."

"But why meet here instead of Washington?" Joe asked.

"Senator Ogilvy came home from D.C. a few days ago because his wife was ill. Remember?"

"Right," Joe replied. He took a sharp turn and headed back toward the warehouse district. "We heard about it the other day."

"The senator knows Dad and put him in charge of security. The techno-thieves arrived and bugged our house."

"Clayton shows up, on their trail," Joe adds. "So they try to kidnap him, but we get in the way."

"Now they've got all the Hardys to deal with," Frank said. "Even our aunt. "

Joe almost laughed. "That's more trouble than any crook can handle. There's the warehouse district ahead. Now what?"

Frank stared out at the desolate-looking area a block ahead. "Stop here," he said. "Somewhere around here there's one of those Dip 'n' Sip dough-nut shops. The ones with the bright orange and red signs."

"The same colors as on the doughnut box those thugs had!" Joe exclaimed.

"We find that shop and see if the clerks can tell us anything," Frank said. "I'm betting our thugs hang around here because that's the only one in town."

It only took the boys a few minutes to find the doughnut shop. The dingy white building stood out against the dark red and brown brick tenements on either side. Soft light glowed through the plate glass windows, and the boys could see a small crowd of people sitting at the tables inside.

"Coffee?" the teenage clerk asked as the Hardys stepped up to the counter. She was slender, with reddish brown hair pulled back in a ponytail. She looked bored. "Our specialty is French Brazilian Mocha Nutty Delight. Buy one and get a free chocolate glazed—"

"Uh . . . no, thanks," Frank replied. He glanced from the skinny waitress to the three or four men sitting around the shop and back to the clerk. "We're looking for a couple of guys we thought might be here," he said.

"Can't help you." The clerk placed one hand on her hip, popped her chewing gum, and glanced past Frank. She saw Joe Hardy and smiled pleasantly. "Next."

Joe returned the smile, eased past Frank, and stepped up to the counter. "Excuse my brother," Joe said. "He's all business."

"No problem," the girl replied, her voice soft and playful.

"We need to find these guys because they offered us a job," Joe explained. He leaned forward a bit.

"And a guy's got to earn some cash so he can go places, *meet people,* and . . . have fun."

Frank rolled his eyes and turned away. Joe would be meeting a lot of hospital personnel if Iola saw this, he thought to himself.

"Who are these guys?" the clerk asked. She didn't seem to care about the three other customers who had stepped up behind Frank and Joe.

"Don't know their names," Joe replied. "They said they worked at one of the warehouses near here. They said if we wanted a job we could always find them here."

"Could we get some service?" one of the annoyed customers asked.

The doughnut clerk ignored him. "What do they look like?" she asked.

Joe described the two thugs. "Sure, I know them." Her face wrinkled into a nasty frown. "Rude, crude, and lousy tippers."

"They work near here?" Frank asked anxiously.

"Sure," the waitress replied without looking at him.

"Glad somebody works around here," one of the customers grumbled.

Again she ignored them. "You probably don't want to work for them," she told Joe. "But we could use another clerk here."

Joe smiled. "They were offering good pay," he said. "More money, more fun."

"They come here twice a day, and the one with the blond hair is a jerk," the waitress announced. "He buys a dozen doughnuts, jelly only. He doesn't share them with his buddy. He doesn't buy coffee, and he never tips."

"I can see why," another customer in line called out.

Joe shifted to the side so she could take some of the orders. She met the customers' comments and irritation with a stony face. But she smiled when she looked at Joe.

Frank glanced at the girl, then at the condition of the doughnut shop. Most of the unoccupied tables were messy. Used napkins and crumbs littered the floor, and the single garbage can was overflowing. He suddenly felt that people eating here were putting their lives in more danger than he and Joe were about to face.

Frank wondered where his father and the congressman were at this very moment. Were they at Senator Ogilvy's home? Possibly. Or had they arranged to meet somewhere else? Either possibility was valid. A secret place would make it harder for anyone to preset any spying devices. But it also made finding them that much harder. Finding the thugs was still their best option, but time was growing short. Frank flashed a concerned look at Joe and indicated his watch. Joe nodded gravely, then his smile returned as he turned to the waitress.

"You were saying," Joe said as she served the last of the customers in line.

"Those guys must work in one of those buildings over there." The waitress pointed out the front window.

Across the street Joe and Frank could see a small cluster of warehouses and storage places—four in all. A single narrow street ran down between them with two on either side.

The two in front were completely dark, but there were a few lights on in the two back buildings.

"Thanks a lot," Joe said, turning to leave.

"Hey, I expect to see you in here a lot more if you get that job." She placed a single finger to her lips.

Joe thought of Iola. Her smile was better. "Believe me," he told the waitress, "if I get a job over there, you'll see me again."

Frank had already started the car when Joe finally jumped in. "That was a sad performance on your part," he told his brother.

Joe shrugged. "Nothing's going to happen," he told Frank. "And besides . . . I did it for Dad."

"What a sacrifice." Frank drove slowly down the narrow street between the four buildings. He and Joe watched for anything that would tell them which building the men might occupy. The dark brick walls were decorated with spray-painted words and pictures. The small parking lots for all four buildings were empty. Nothing seemed to move, and there were no apparent signs that anyone was around until they reach the far side of the fourth building.

Frank had driven behind it to turn around and cruise back up the street. Tucked in an alley behind the building, away from the street, the boys spotted the Land Rover. "Bingo!" Frank whispered.

The vehicle was parked next to a Dumpster. Its back door was open, and the Hardys could see a few small boxes in the back. There was a steel door a few feet past the Dumpster. A single outdoor lamp hung overhead, casting a harsh white light on the stained and dirty alley floor. Frank quickly cut his headlights and cruised past the Land Rover down to the far end of the alley. He turned the corner of the building and stopped.

"What now?" Joe asked. "Do we take 'em or go for help?"

"Big problem," Frank said. He squeezed the steering wheel hard with both hands. "We can't use our cell phones to call anyone because the crooks might pick up the call. And if we leave, they might get away."

"Even though the hatch was open, we're not sure they're both in there," Joe said. "Let's check that out first, then decide what to do next."

Just as the boys opened their car doors, they heard the sound of a car engine back down the alley. By the time they crept to the corner of the building and peeked around, the motor had been shut off. Frank and Joe peered down the alleyway and noticed that the metal door near the Dumpster was just swinging shut. Parked next to the Land Rover was a sleek black sedan with tinted windows.

"That's an expensive piece of machinery," Joe commented. "It's also familiar."

"Sure is," Frank agreed. "So we know that the third man is probably here, too."

Just then, the metal door opened and the dark-skinned thug came out. He walked to the back of the Land Rover and slid out a large box halfway. Before picking it up, he opened the top and rummaged through the contents.

The metal door swung open again, and his partner stuck his head out.

"It's our doughnut-loving thug," Joe whispered.

"Come on, Rudy," the man called out in a harsh whisper. "The boss says it's going down in ten minutes."

"Keep your shirt on, Nick," Rudy replied. He picked up the open box with one hand and shut the door with the other. A few seconds later he was back inside the warehouse.

"That settles it," Joe said through gritted teeth. "We don't have the time to go for help. They're going to steal something from Dad and his client right now."

"Okay, let's split up," Frank suggested. "Maybe we can find out what they're going to do, and how."

"Then we can take 'em down!" Joe insisted.

"Or go for help," Frank said. He noticed an open window near a stack of crates, not far from where they were hiding. "I'll go in that way, and you try to find another way in around the far side of the building."

Joe nodded, and Frank watched his younger brother creep down the alley past the metal door. When Joe reached the far corner of the building, he glanced back at Frank and gave him a high sign. Frank's stomach tightened as Joe disappeared around that corner. He had no idea what was down there, and he didn't like the idea that they had so little information. How many were there, in total? What were they actually about to do?

Frank began moving cautiously down the alley toward the open window he had spotted. Only the overhead lamp cast any light into the alley.

Frank knew he and Joe had been on their own before, but something about fighting cyber-ghosts spooked him more than he wanted to admit. They had invaded his home and threatened his family and friends. Their activities made them seem all-seeing and all-powerful.

Frank reached the window. A foul odor rose from the stack of crates and boxes next to it. The boxes were covered with dark greasy stains, and rubble was scattered all around them.

Frank turned his attention to the window. The sill was six feet up, and the window was tall, narrow, and opened inward. I can probably just squeeze through, he told himself.

He reached up and placed his hands on the gritty stone windowsill. Just as he was about to climb up, Frank felt a blow to his ribs. The punch caused his knees to go weak. Before he could recover, a powerful arm locked around his throat and began to squeeze the air—the very life—from his body.

15 Subject Neutralized

Frank shot his elbow back into his attacker's midsection three times in rapid succession. It hit rock-hard abdominal muscles and barely caused the man to grunt. His grip tightened on Frank's throat, and the older Hardy brother thought it might be all over—until he heard a loud thud.

Slowly the man's grip released, and his arm fell away from Frank, following its owner down to the concrete.

Gasping for air, Frank turned to see his brother standing over the unconscious form of Rudy. Joe held what was left of a wooden two-by-four in his hand.

Joe smiled. "From the arm that gave our softball team sixteen home runs last season," he whispered.

Joe helped Frank to his feet and away from the window.

"How'd you know I was in trouble?" Frank gasped.

"Lucky," Joe replied. "The other side of this building is a solid brick wall. No windows or doors. So I came back this way, figuring to follow you in, and there was Rudy. The rest is poetry."

Frank recovered quickly, and the boys used their belts to secure Rudy and hide him behind the crates. "What was that you stuffed in his mouth?" Joe asked as they approached the window again.

Frank looked at the rags and muck in the stack of crates and trash. "You don't want to know."

Joe shuddered, then followed Frank in through the window.

They landed quietly in the cavernous darkness. It's like some weird cave, Joe thought to himself.

The inside was one large room about the size of a city block. Pipes, crates, and pillars of varying sizes created strange structures and shadows along the floor. Chains, pulleys, and cables hung from the ceilings and tracks like stalactites. Moonlight barely filtered in through the dirty wire mesh windows, which ran along three sides of the building. A series of catwalks crisscrossed the two-story building. They gave access to metal platforms suspended above old and now discarded machinery.

The only electric light that was on seemed to be focused in the center of the room. But the boys couldn't see anything because of the machinery and crates stacked here and there. Some stacks rose fifteen feet in the air.

Joe checked the dial on his luminous watch. They had only five minutes left in which to stop the thieves. Slowly they crept toward the source of the light and soon came to the center of the room. It was a wide-open space, thirty feet across. In the center stood a metal platform about ten feet square and eight feet high. Two sets of metal stairs rose to the top of the platform, connected to metal railings that ran almost all the way around.

Positioned on the platform were two short tables and two swivel chairs. Desk lamps were clamped to each table. A complex array of electronic equipment had been stacked on the table and was wired to two keyboards and computer monitors. The screens glowed a soft blue. Two men, their backs to Frank and Joe, were working hard at them. A third man, Nick, was standing near them, munching away on a jelly doughnut.

Frank's eyes followed a coaxial cable that ran up from the equipment, past the catwalk above, and out through the skylight.

"I bet there's a miniature satellite dish on the roof," he whispered to Joe. "They capture the information they want, then beam it to another satellite dish."

"Except that one is in outer space, and from there they can beam the information anywhere in the world." Joe's face tightened with anger. "And this time they're after our national defense secrets."

"Worth millions to any foreign power."

"Well, they should have stuck to corporate secrets," Joe said. He clinched his fists. "Let's do this."

Frank grabbed Joe's arm. "Wait."

"Congressman Reynolds and Senator Ogilvy just put through their call to Washington," one of the two men on the platform said. "You ready?"

Frank and Joe recognized the voice.

The second man leaned back in his chair and clasped his hands behind his head. "I'm always ready, Harlan," he said.

Harlan Dean jumped up, grabbed the man by his shirtfront, and pulled him to his feet. "This deal is worth fifty million dollars to me, and I won't let you louse it up!"

"It's cool, it's cool," the scrawny man pleaded. "I'm ready. Honest."

"We've got to cut the connection before they begin transmitting," Frank told his brother.

Desperately they looked around for some way to sabotage the operation. Frank's gaze stopped on the metal door, and a plan began to form. Joe's plan had also crystallized. He had spotted the stairs that led up to the catwalk.

The boys quickly discussed their ideas, then separated.

Cautiously Frank slipped out through the metal door and approached the Land Rover. As he remembered, the windows were rolled down, so he knew the perimeter alarm was not on. Frank slipped inside the vehicle and went to work.

Inside the warehouse, Joe had to move more cautiously and slowly to reach the stairs unheard. He hoped the old metal would not creak or rattle as he mounted the steps in the semidarkness.

"The Security Council is on the line," the scrawny technician told Harlan Dean. "They're asking how Ogilvy's wife is."

Joe eased up one flight of steps and stopped when Nick started to leave the platform.

"Where are you going?" Harlan asked him.

"Rudy's been gone too long," Nick replied. "How long's it take to get coffee? The doughnut place is just across the street."

"Stay put," Dean snarled. "We're going live in two minutes, and I don't want any foul-ups. "

Nick grumbled as he resumed his place on the platform. Harlan Dean sat down at the second keyboard and began clicking away.

Joe looked at his watch. Frank would be ready in less than thirty seconds. He had to get into position. Moving as quickly as he dared, Joe eased out onto the catwalk and moved forward inch by inch.

"They're beginning to discuss the U.S. defense package," the technician announced.

"Actually," Harlan said, chuckling, "they're about to discuss my financial security for the rest of my life."

"How'd you explain not being there when the talks started?" Nick asked.

"Security sweep," Dean replied. "I'm out cruising the neighborhood for any random transmission signals."

"Smart," Nick replied.

"No," Harlan Dean said as he typed a command on the keyboard. "Genius. Let's do it." He hit the return key.

The garage door exploded inward, and a thirty-thousand-dollar Land Rover roared through it and into the warehouse. Crates and boxes flew in every direction.

The technician fell backward from his chair, striking his head on the hard metal railing. He didn't move. Nick stumbled into some of the equipment, then leaped from the platform, rushing toward the disturbance.

Instantly, Joe Hardy leaped forward along the catwalk, grabbed the cable, and yanked it with all his strength. The cable broke loose from the roof and dropped to the platform below.

Harlan Dean saw it and reached for the service revolver on his belt as he spun around. The security chief looked up in time to see Joe Hardy dropping toward him from the platform above. The younger

Hardy landed on Dean with tremendous force, slamming the man to the floor and knocking him out.

"Thanks for the padding, buddy," Joe said. He leaped to his feet and began disabling the equipment.

Nick reached the totaled Land Rover, fully expecting to find his partner slumped behind the seat. "Rudy! Rudy, what's wrong with—"

Frank stepped from behind some large pipes and lashed out with a karate kick to Nick's knee. The man went down but tried to get up again. Frank followed through with a powerful elbow to the man's jaw. Nick groaned but did not move.

"You okay, Joe?" Frank called out.

"No problem!"

Suddenly the alley outside was alive with the flashing lights and sounds of people leaping from cars and running.

Joe and Frank whirled toward the noise, fearful that more of Harlan Dean's associates had arrived.

They were happy to see the police come through the wrecked doorway, led by their father. Close behind him were Clayton Silvers and Aunt Gertrude.

Joe leaped down from the platform and ran toward Frank.

"Are you boys all right?" Fenton asked as he reached them.

"Sure, Dad," Joe replied. "But how—"

"How many times have I told you boys not to go

putting yourselves in danger?" Aunt Gertrude scolded. "I—uh—we were so worried about you."

"We're sorry, Aunt Gertrude," Frank apologized. "But how'd you guys find us?"

"I've been suspicious of Harlan for a couple of days," Fenton told them. He watched the police run past them and begin to secure Dean and his associates. "Right after I found out he'd asked the hotel manager to keep an eye on Clayton—even before the break-in."

"You knew about that?" Joe exclaimed.

"Earlier tonight I guessed that he was the security consultant for several of the places that were robbed," Clayton Silvers added. "And then I put it all together, and it was the only thing that made any sense. I contacted the police, who contacted your father. The police put out an APB on my car, which you boys were driving. Once it was located we were golden. Your dad had hooked up with your aunt back at the house—and here we all are."

"So, you didn't need us on this case," Frank said somewhat disappointed.

"On the contrary," Clayton said. "We had no idea how he was going to do it, or where."

"If you boys hadn't nailed this location," Fenton admitted, "some serious defense information might have leaked out."

A police officer brought Harlan Dean over to Fenton and the group. The bruised and disgruntled security chief glared at Fenton and Clayton, then glanced at Frank and Joe. "I didn't figure on you two," he grumbled.

"No one ever does," Fenton told him coldly. He then turned to his sister. "We Hardys are a persistent breed."

"I hear that," Clayton agreed. "Loud and clear."

"We sank your career, but good," Harlan snarled.

"Or just gave me a Pulitzer prize-winning story," Clayton replied calmly. "Gotcha!"

"Hold that pose!"

The group saw a flash go off, then turned to see Darryl running up to them. He snapped another picture.

"Front-page stuff!" he exclaimed. "My ticket to fame!"

Clayton Silvers laughed. "Be careful what you wish for, brother," he said. "Be real careful."

16 All Clear

The next morning the sky was clear with large billowy clouds that reflected a lemon yellow sun.

In the Hardys' kitchen, the sweet aroma of waffles, bacon, coffee, and fresh strawberries mingled with the sounds of cheerful talk and laughter. It was a breakfast party. Family and friends were together to celebrate a great victory.

Fenton Hardy sat at the kitchen table with Tony Prito, Phil Cohen, Darryl, Callie, and Iola. Fenton was savoring his first cup of morning coffee while the kids were enjoying their second helping of waffles.

Joe and Frank were eating their breakfast standing

at the kitchen counter. They exchanged jokes and remarks with their friends while Clayton Silvers helped Aunt Gertrude serve more food.

"We could all sit at the dining room table," Aunt Gertrude commented as she poured Phil another glass of orange juice. "There's more than enough room for everyone."

"We're fine here," Phil mumbled through a mouthful of food.

Besides," Clayton added. "You know kitchens are warm and friendly," he said. "And I can't think of a better place for this group to gather." He raised his cup of coffee to the Hardys. "You really came through for me. I can never thank you enough."

"You could stay in touch more." Gertrude Hardy gave Clayton a stern sideward glance. "Besides," she continued, "I have to admit it felt good to right an injustice. Very exciting."

Suddenly she caught the look in her brother's eyes. "But I certainly do not want to go through it again," she added quickly.

"I don't think we'll have to," Fenton told his sister. "Harlan and his gang will be inside for a long time."

"Why'd he do it?" Tony Prito asked, just before gulping down another mouthful of food.

"Money," Clayton replied matter-of-factly.

"But he was making a bundle as a security consultant," Iola said.

"Maybe he felt it wasn't enough," Joe offered.

"Well, he's still got clients," Clayton told the group. "The Justice Department, FBI, CIA, NSA—all those alphabet agencies want the names, places, and dates of every buyer he's done business with."

"Sounds like there'll be indictments everywhere," Fenton said.

"Every one of them deserves it." Aunt Gertrude poured herself another cup of coffee. "They were making others suffer, and that is inexcusable."

Joe moved next to his aunt and placed an arm around her shoulders. "We've never heard you talk like this," he told her. "In fact, I learned a lot of new things about you."

"And?" Aunt Gertrude said without looking at him.

"We just wonder how you can be so strict with us when you had a wild side, too."

"You and Frank and your father try to help people," Gertrude Hardy said slowly. "I believe in that. It's what we Hardys do and have always done. But you boys attract so much danger . . . that I worry. I guess I can't explain it better than that."

Frank and Joe remembered the story Clayton had told them. "We understand," Frank told her. "Really we do."

"So do we," Callie Shaw added.

"I just want you to be careful, that's all," Aunt Gertrude suddenly snapped. She began grabbing up empty cups and plates.

"I'm still eating," Phil called out as she picked up

147

his plate. There was still half a waffle sitting in the middle.

"Sorry," Aunt Gertrude mumbled.

"So what are you going to do now, Mr. Silvers?" Darryl asked.

The reporter casually leaned back against the kitchen door jamb and held up a copy of the *Bayport Times*. In bold, black type, the headline read, "Tech Thieves Off Line," by Clayton Silvers. Darryl received credit for an assist.

"This story hit in five major cities," Clayton announced. "Not to mention radio, TV, and the Web. I had offers from all of them, including an offer to have my old job back."

"Which one will you take?" Iola asked.

Clayton smiled. "I have no clue," he admitted. "I might choose to stay freelance and write a book."

"You'd never settle down anywhere," Aunt Gertrude said, teasing. "You'd miss the action."

"Well, whatever I decide, Spitfire"—everyone in the room chuckled, including Aunt Gertrude—"it sure feels good to have a choice."

"I know we'll be seeing more articles by you soon," Frank told Clayton.

"Yeah, and I hope we'll be hearing more stories about Aunt Gertrude. Like the—"

"Don't you dare, Joseph Hardy." Aunt Gertrude began chasing Joe as he playfully dashed out into the garden.

"There are a lot of thieves out there, Frank," Clayton said as he watched Joe and Aunt Gertrude. "Someone's got to take them down. Someone clever like me . . . and *crazy* like you Hardys."

Do your younger brothers and sisters want to read books like yours?

Let them know there are books just for *them!*

They can join Nancy Drew and her best friends as they collect clues and solve mysteries in

THE

NANCY DREW

NOTEBOOKS®

Starting with

#1 The Slumber Party Secret

#2 The Lost Locket

#3 The Secret Santa

#4 Bad Day for Ballet

AND

Meet up with suspense and mystery in The Hardy Boys® are: The Clues Brothers™

Starting with

#1 The Gross Ghost Mystery

#2 The Karate Clue

#3 First Day, Worst Day

#4 Jump Shot Detectives

THE CLUES BROTHERS™

A MINSTREL® BOOK

Published by Pocket Books

2324

BRUCE COVILLE'S

The fascinating and hilarious adventures of
the world's first purple sixth grader!

I WAS A SIXTH GRADE ALIEN

THE ATTACK OF THE TWO-INCH TEACHER

I LOST MY GRANDFATHER'S BRAIN

PEANUT BUTTER LOVERBOY

ZOMBIES OF THE SCIENCE FAIR

DON'T FRY MY VEEBLAX!

TOO MANY ALIENS

SNATCHED FROM EARTH

THERE'S AN ALIEN IN MY BACKPACK

THE REVOLT OF THE MINATURE MUTANTS

A MINSTREL® BOOK

Published by Pocket Books

2304-05

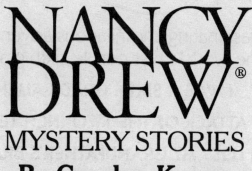

2313